"Our reputations are ruined!"

"You're a senator," Paula continued hotly. "Can't you call that columnist and make him retract the statement?" She glared at Matthew accusingly. "I've taken great pains since Richard's death to preserve a good reputation, and now..."

"Sit down, Paula!" Matthew's voice rang out with authority. "I have a solution," he told her in a gentler tone. "We'll get married."

Married! A nasty item in a gossip column was one thing, a lifetime commitment without love quite another. "Wouldn't it be simpler to just call off the whole arrangement?"

"Is that what you want, to go back to dealing with your sister's interference, fending off passes?"

Paula thought back to the bleak days before Matthew had come into her life, and she knew she didn't want to go back to that dreary emptiness....

Books by Rosemary Hammond

HARLEQUIN PRESENTS
802—THE HABIT OF LOVING

HARLEQUIN ROMANCE
2601—FULL CIRCLE
2655—TWO DOZEN RED ROSES
2674—THE SCENT OF HIBISCUS

These books may be available at your local bookseller.

Don't miss any of our special offers. Write to us at the following address for information on our newest releases.

Harlequin Reader Service
P.O. Box 52040, Phoenix, AZ 85072-2040
Canadian address: P.O. Box 2800, Postal Station A,
5170 Yonge St., Willowdale, Ont. M2N 6J3

ROSEMARY HAMMOND

the habit of loving

Harlequin Books

TORONTO • NEW YORK • LONDON
AMSTERDAM • PARIS • SYDNEY • HAMBURG
STOCKHOLM • ATHENS • TOKYO • MILAN

Harlequin Presents first edition July 1985
ISBN 0-373-10802-8

Original hardcover edition published in 1985
by Mills & Boon Limited

CHAPTER ONE

PAULA stood patiently in the receiving line wondering once again why she allowed her sister to talk her into attending these dreary affairs. The line inched slowly forward, each one of the three hundred or so people at the gala reception anxious to shake hands with the new senator from Maryland.

After the tasteless meal there had been speeches that seemed to drone on for hours. As usual, Paula paid no attention to who was speaking or what was said. Through long practice, she had polished the ability to tune herself out of these political functions to a fine art.

She felt David's arm come around her waist now, pulling her towards him. She flinched, stiffened and gave him a swift icy frown. The arm dropped away.

'For God's sake, Paula,' he muttered under his breath, 'that wasn't a pass. Relax.'

'I'm perfectly relaxed,' she said coolly, 'so long as you keep your hands to yourself.'

David raised his light blue eyes heavenward in exasperation. Paula knew he was fighting anger. His masculine ego was bruised by her rejection. She didn't care. She'd made it perfectly plain to David in a hundred ways that she didn't want to be touched. Not that way, at any rate.

He was shaking his blond head now, smiling, his intrinsic good nature and sunny disposition winning out over resentment at her rebuff.

'I don't know why I put up with you,' he said in a tone of mock resignation.

'Of course you do, David.' Her voice was brisk. 'Margaret bullies you into it.'

He laughed. It was true, Paula thought, moving a few steps forward in line, and David knew it as well as she did. Her sister wielded immense power in Washington's social world, not only because she was the wife of one of the President's top aides and had seemingly unlimited money to spend, but through the force of her own personality.

'There's some truth to that,' David admitted ruefully. 'Your sister is a formidable woman. Why she isn't president beats me.'

'Oh, give her time,' Paula countered drily. 'She's only thirty-six, barely over the minimum age to qualify.'

'Speak of the devil,' David murmured. 'Brace yourself.'

They had almost reached the head of the line, now, and Paula could see Margaret's flaming red head, hear the strident high-pitched voice as she greeted the people in front of them.

At last, Paula said to herself with a sigh. She could go home soon. She hadn't wanted to come at all, but as usual, Margaret had overridden her feeble objections. Her sister had energetically embarked on a rigorous campaign six months ago to, as she put it, pull Paula out of her gloomy shell, and once Margaret made up her mind to something, she was irresistible.

Ten years older than Paula, she had been more like a second mother to her when their own mother died. They were as different as two women could possibly be, Paula thought now as the sharp hazel eyes fastened on her. Margaret was every inch the supremely confident extrovert with her easy, outgoing manner, while Paula, more intense and reserved by nature, had withdrawn even more into her own private world after Richard's death.

'There you are, darling,' Margaret shrieked at her, as though she had half-expected her to vanish as soon as her back was turned. 'And David. How nice. What a handsome couple you make.'

Paula sighed. Margaret acted as though she and David were romantically involved and that Margaret herself hadn't engineered the whole thing. Poor David. As a very junior congressman from Massachusetts, he couldn't very well refuse to be pressed into service as her escort when Margaret commanded.

'Now, there's going to be dancing later in the ballroom,' Margaret went on. 'You'll be at our table.' Before Paula's objection could reach her ears, Margaret had turned to David. 'You *will* see to it that she stays, won't you, David?' Her tone was firm.

'Of course,' David murmured.

'Now,' Margaret said, turning to her husband, 'William will introduce you to Senator Stratton.'

She dismissed them with a look, her bright smile now fastened on the people behind them in line, her hand outstretched in greeting.

'Hello, William,' Paula said, smiling up at her brother-in-law.

He was a big bear of a man, heavy-set, red-faced, with a shiny bald head fringed with grey, and one of the kindest men Paula had ever known. He obviously adored his vibrant red-headed wife and had been almost like a father to Paula.

'Paula, my dear.' She lifted her face for his warm brotherly peck. 'How nice to see you. And

David,' he added, shaking hands with the younger man. 'I'd like you both to meet Senator Stratton.'

Paula glanced at the tall man standing beside William. He was still speaking to the people ahead of them, and his dark head was turned slightly away so that his face was in profile. Throughout the dinner and the speeches, Paula hadn't paid any attention to him. She and David had sat at the back, far from the head table, and she had only a dim recollection of a tall man with a deep voice giving one more boring speech.

Now, really looking at him for the first time, Paula drew in her breath sharply. He was so much like Richard that for a moment it could have been her dead husband standing there before her. Then he turned to face her, and the illusion was shattered. The hair was darker than Richard's, coarse and crisp instead of smooth and silky, the features more prominent, the expression more forbidding. Richard had been a handsome man, a beautiful man, Paula had often thought, with melting brown eyes and a warm friendly smile that had lit up the world for her.

This man's face looked as though it had been carved in granite. There was only the shadow of a polite smile on the thin straight lips, and all resemblance to Richard vanished completely when she looked into those stony grey eyes.

'My sister-in-law, Paula Waring,' she heard William say to him now, as if from an immense distance. 'And David Wyatt, our junior congressman from Massachusetts. Senator Matthew Stratton.'

Paula held out a hand stiffly, touched his briefly, then withdrew it. 'Mrs Waring,' he murmured, giving her a brief cool glance, then turning to David. Paula smiled politely at him, murmured a greeting and moved on. She was filled with a vague resentment towards this aloof stranger. Because he wasn't Richard, she wondered, or because of his unfriendly manner?

As David guided her through the crush of people towards the ballroom of the hotel, she forgot all about Senator Stratton and wondered how soon she could slip away without calling down Margaret's wrath. They had been near the end of the receiving line, and already she could hear the orchestra playing in the ballroom and see that several couples were out on the floor dancing.

The waiter led them to William's table, placed prominently at the very edge of the dance floor. It was a table for eight, Paula noticed, but no one else was sitting there.

'Would you care to dance?' David asked.

'No, thanks, David. Not right now.'

He seated her at the table. 'How about a drink?'

She nodded. 'All right. Campari and soda, please.'

David gave their order to the hovering waiter and sat down beside her. 'Well, what did you think of our new senator?' he asked.

She shrugged. 'Not much. He doesn't have a very scintillating personality. I wonder how he ever got elected.'

David laughed. 'Oh, he's Maryland's great white hope. Comes from a prominent family there with money in the background.'

Paula smiled. David's own family had settled in New England before the Revolutionary War and by all accounts owned half the State.

Their drinks arrived then and David signed for them.

'You mean he bought his way into the Senate?' Paula asked over her drink.

'Oh, no,' David assured her hurriedly. 'Nothing like that. He was involved in State politics for a number of years, and while he doesn't have a politician's typical gladhanding manner, he's a sound man, quite capable, and, I hear, immensely popular in his own constituency.'

'I'll take your word for it,' Paula said drily. The subject bored her. All she had on her mind was how soon she could decently get away.

'Oh, oh,' David said in a low voice. 'I see your sister and her party bearing down on us. If you don't want another lecture, I suggest you make the supreme sacrifice and dance just once with me. Then you can safely leave.' His tone was faintly mocking.

Paula gave him a swift look and frowned. He made her sound rude, almost boorish.

'David . . .' she began.

He stood up abruptly and held out a hand. 'Come on.'

They danced sedately to the old-fashioned dance music. It was a conservative crowd, predominantly middle-aged. Power in government came late in life as a rule, and this gathering included many of the more prominent figures in Washington's political hierarchy.

Paula was grateful to see that David was content to keep a small space between them as they danced. On the first occasion Margaret had pressed him into service as her escort, he had plastered his body against hers when they danced and made passes at her so persistently, that finally Paula had threatened to take a cab home and never go out with him again.

His ego could take it, she thought now, glancing up at him. He was considered a prime catch in a city where women outnumbered men almost two to one, and had been spoiled by Washington's society hostesses from the day he set foot in the nation's capital. Not only were his blond good looks appealing, but the money in his family's background was a powerful attraction.

'You look lovely, as always, Paula,' he said to her now as he caught her smile and held it. 'That dress suits you. What do you call the colour? It just matches your eyes.'

'Thank you, David.' Her voice was cool. 'I haven't a clue what the colour is. Blue-green, I guess.'

'That sounds so pedestrian,' he objected, 'especially for a fashion illustrator. It must have a more romantic name than that.'

She laughed. 'If there is one, the store hasn't told me about it. Maybe I can create one myself. How about aquamarine? Is that fancy enough?'

David's blue eyes were warm. 'You're beautiful when you smile, Paula. You should do it more often.' He reached up a hand and touched her smooth black hair, brushing away the heavy fringe that fell across her forehead.

Immediately she stiffened. The smile vanished, and a determined lift of her chin warned David that he was on the verge of crossing her carefully erected boundaries.

At that moment the music stopped. David dropped his hands to his sides, and Paula took a short step back from him. They walked back to the table in silence, David's hand lightly holding her elbow.

The table was full by now. Margaret was

holding court at one end, and William was deep in conversation with Senator Stratton and a man from the Justice Department at the other.

'There you are,' Margaret called to her. 'I was afraid you'd gone home.' Her voice was accusing.

'No, Margaret,' Paula replied wearily, as David seated her next to her sister. 'As you can see, I'm still here. David and I have been dancing. Surely I get high marks for that.'

Margaret darted her a suspicious look, then brightened. 'That's wonderful.' She turned to the beautiful blonde woman at her other side. 'You know Michele Lathrop, don't you, Paula?'

'Of course. How are you Michele?' Paula knew her more by reputation than personal friendship. A thirtyish divorcée whose father was a power in the State Department, her name had been linked with every prominent eligible man in Washington at one time or another.

Paula surmised that she must be with Senator Stratton, since Margaret went on to introduce the other woman at the table as Mrs Pittinger, whose husband was talking to William and the senator.

The music started up again, and Mr and Mrs Pittinger moved out on to the floor. Then David asked Michele to dance, and Paula sighed with relief. Michele Lathrop was far more David's cup of tea than she was.

She saw David's arms come around the tall blonde, one palm flat against her bare back, pulling her closely to him. Michele seemed to melt against him, her hands meeting at the back of his neck, a provocative smile on her wide mouth as she gazed up at him.

'Jealous, darling?' Margaret asked.

Paula's eyes widened and she turned to give her

sister an incredulous look. 'Of David? You must be joking.'

Margaret forced a bitter smile and sighed. 'Of course. I forgot myself for a moment.' She leaned towards Paula and muttered, 'What does it take, sister dear, to interest you in a man?'

'Margaret, will you please give it up?' Paula pleaded with her. 'How can I convince you that I simply *can't* get interested in a man?'

'You mean you don't want to,' Margaret accused. 'You refuse.'

'Well?' Paula spread her arms. 'What's the difference? Can't or won't, it amounts to the same thing.'

William and Senator Stratton had risen to their feet now, duty winning out over their absorption in their conversation, and stood over the two women. Paula hoped they hadn't overheard Margaret's tart comments.

'Mrs Chandler,' the tall dark man was saying to Margaret, 'Would you care to dance?'

Margaret looked up at him. 'Oh, I don't think so, thank you. My arthritis is acting up. Why don't you dance with Paula?'

Paula could have murdered her on the spot. Arthritis, indeed! Margaret hadn't had an ache or a pain or a day's illness in her life. The germs wouldn't dare. She glanced up ruefully at Senator Stratton and opened her mouth to refuse, but by now he had crossed to her side of the table and was holding out a hand to her.

There was nothing for it but to give in gracefully, she thought as she took his hand and rose to her feet. She wondered if this tall dark man had six hands she'd have to parry. He looked the type, she thought, cool, confident, aware of his good looks.

She needn't have worried. He held her loosely, without warmth, and seemed vaguely preoccupied, not even making an attempt to strike up a conversation. More than that, she thought as they continued to dance in silence, he seemed to be as bored as she was. Damn Margaret, she thought, for foisting me off on the poor man.

'I'm sorry,' she said stiffly at last.

He jerked his attention back to her, frowning slightly. 'I beg your pardon?'

'I said I was sorry,' she repeated more loudly. 'About Margaret pushing you into dancing with me. She's inclined to manipulate.'

A fleeting smile crossed the hard features. 'Yes, I've noticed. It's probably what makes her such a successful hostess. Sometimes people need manipulating.'

'You might be right,' she agreed, surprised at his perceptiveness, 'but it gets a little wearying when you're related to her.'

He nodded gravely. 'I can imagine. I couldn't help overhearing the tail end of your – conversation.'

Paula reddened. 'Margaret never lets up,' she muttered, horribly embarrassed.

He shrugged. 'I know the feeling. I'm a victim of the same kind of thing myself.'

She gave him a sharp look. Was this a new approach? 'Really?' she asked dubiously.

He nodded. 'I've found the best way to handle it is to just go along with it. There's no harm in it, and you meet some interesting people.'

Paula thought this over as they finished the dance. He might be right. Certainly it did no good to fight it. Margaret was as determined to matchmake as Paula was to resist it. Perhaps this resistance only whetted her sister's appetite.

She wondered why Matthew Stratton had found it necessary to learn to deal with matchmaking attempts. Was he just a confirmed bachelor? A womaniser who wanted his freedom to play the field?

Somehow she doubted that. She'd never danced with a man who seemed so unaware of her as a woman. He could be holding a plaster mannequin for all the response she evoked in him. And during their short conversation, there had been no hint of teasing innuendo or flirting in his tone.

Perhaps he only likes blondes, she thought, as he led her back to the table and seated her next to David. She watched him go over to Michele and lean down to ask her to dance. When the gorgeous blonde smiled seductively up at him, rose to her feet and put an arm intimately through his, Paula saw that his expression remained the same; serious, remote, indifferent.

Later, dancing with William, she saw them on the dance floor. They made a striking couple, she thought, he so tall and dark, she so blonde and fair. Her hands were linked around his neck, and Paula could see that she was pressing herself up against him. Even at such intimate contact, however, the dark grey eyes were cold, his whole bearing detached and remote.

He seemed to be preoccupied, his mind a million miles away, and Paula couldn't help wondering what it was, what inner obsession filled his mind so completely that he could quite easily resist the charms of the beautiful woman who seemed to be offering herself to him on a plate.

When the telephone rang early the next morning, Paula knew before she answered it that it would be

Margaret calling. Not only was she expecting a dressing down from her sister, but the phone seemed to have a special ring to it when Margaret called, shriller somehow, and more insistent.

'Well,' came the imperious voice, 'what have you got to say for yourself?'

'Margaret, I'm trying to get some work done. I've got a deadline on these illustrations and have to get them to the newspaper before noon today.'

'Oh, bother the drawings. What did you mean sneaking out last night?'

'That's easy for you to say,' Paula countered, ignoring the last question on the frail hope that the best defence was a good offence. 'You sit out there in Virginia in the lap of luxury, while I have to slave away earning a living.'

'You wouldn't have to earn a living if you'd just get married again,' was the tart reply. 'Now, answer my question.'

Paula sighed and glanced out the window at the rain slashing against the glass panes. She'd have to come up with a good answer or Margaret would never let her get back to work.

'I wasn't feeling well,' she said weakly. It wasn't really a lie. She'd been sleeping badly for months and barely picked at her food.

'I knew it, I knew it,' came her sister's triumphant cry. 'I've been after you for weeks to go to a doctor. You look terrible. You're way too thin, and have no colour at all.'

'Thanks a lot. You're making me feel much better. I don't care how I look anyway.' Tears threatened, and she swallowed hastily, blinking them back.

There was silence on the line while Paula collected herself. Margaret was obviously chewing over her last remarks.

'Paula,' she said at last in a softer tone, 'I want you to make an appointment to see Dr Banks today. I'm worried about you. You've got to snap out of it. Richard's been dead almost a year, now, and. . . .'

'I don't want to talk about that,' Paula interrupted firmly.

Margaret sighed dramatically. 'All right. Have it your way.' She paused, then went on in a brisk voice. 'Will you call Dr Banks, or shall I do it for you?'

Paula knew she was quite capable of forcing their old family doctor to come in person to the apartment, and decided that it would be simpler for everyone if she agreed.

'All right. I'll call tomorrow.'

'Today!' came the firm rejoinder.

'Today,' Paula agreed, just to get rid of her. She simply had to get to work. She found it hard enough to concentrate her attention on fashion drawings in her depressed state without having to contend with Margaret.

'What did you think of Matthew Stratton?' Margaret asked in an elaborately casual tone.

'I didn't think anything about him. Why should I?'

'No reason. I just thought you and he had a lot in common.'

Oh, no, Paula groaned inwardly, not more matchmaking. 'Oh?' came the guarded reply. 'In what way?'

'Just that he's as slippery as you are. Mamie Burch, in Baltimore, knows him and his family quite well. She told me he was a widower who didn't go out much, but seemed to like blondes. I went to a great deal of trouble to get Michele

Lathrop for him last night, and he ducked out not long after you vanished.' Her voice trembled with indignation. 'David very kindly offered to take her home.'

'Well, that worked out all right, then.' Paula was infinitely bored with the conversation and only wanted to get to work.

'No, it didn't,' Margaret snapped. 'You know I wanted David for you.'

'Well, Michele is welcome to him. She's more his type than I am anyway. Listen, Margaret, I've got to get to work. Talk to you later.'

Paula hung up the telephone and sat at her desk staring out at the rain for several minutes, realising it would soon be November; a dreary month in Washington, and that it would get worse. Soon the ice and snow would appear.

A familiar wave of depression began to creep insidiously through her. It would be her first winter without Richard, and she didn't think she could bear it. She had always hated the cold, the short days, the icy streets and bitter winds off the Potomac. Only Richard's sunny smile and laughing dark eyes, so full of love, had made it tolerable.

The apartment they had shared during their short marriage still seemed to be full of him. She still listened for his footstep in the hall, the turn of his key in the lock, his cheerful voice calling her name.

Oh, Richard, she thought, as the tears welled up out of control, why did you leave me? She put her head down on the desk and sobbed brokenly.

When it was over, she felt a little calmer, but drained of the small energy she had. I can't go on like this, she thought. I can't work. I can barely function. For the first time, she felt a prick of serious alarm at her condition.

She thought of her promise to Margaret to see Dr Banks. As usual, her sister was right. She made herself look up the number, and slowly dialled.

'Well, you're healthy enough,' Dr Banks said after the thorough examination was over. 'Just a little run down.'

It had been a week before she could get in to see him, and now, after being poked and jabbed and stuck with an assortment of long needles, it was only to hear what she already knew. Of course she was run down, she thought irritably. Who wouldn't be?

Dr Banks gave her a long appraising look over the top of his rimless glasses. 'How long has Richard been gone, now, Paula?'

'Almost a year,' was the curt reply. She met his gaze stonily.

'A boating accident, wasn't it?'

'Yes,' she said shortly. 'On Chesapeake Bay.'

He shook his head. 'Terrible thing. A fine young man. He worked for your sister's husband, didn't he?'

Paula nodded and shifted uncomfortably in her chair. Didn't he realise how she hated to discuss it? She half rose to leave.

'Well, if that's all . . .' she began.

'No,' he said sharply. 'That isn't all. Sit down.' Startled by his tone, she obeyed. 'You know you can't go on like this, Paula,' he said in a kinder voice. 'I'm going to give you a prescription.' He scribbled on a pad, tore off a sheet and handed it to her. 'Just vitamins and minerals. And I want you to get some exercise. Do you jog? Play tennis? Swim?'

Paula shook her head slowly at each question.

Then she remembered. 'There is a swimming pool in the basement of the apartment block. I just never thought to use it.'

'Well, I think you'd better start.' He stood up. 'You'll be all right. You're a healthy girl. How old are you?' He glanced down at her chart. 'Twenty-six?' She nodded. 'Just a girl,' he said cheerfully. 'Too young to grieve like this. You have your whole life ahead of you.'

No, I don't, she thought as she thanked him politely and walked out of the office. No one seemed to understand, and she was tired of explaining that for all intents and purposes, her life ended the day Richard's body was recovered from that stormy sea.

Even so, she thought, as she let herself into her Georgetown apartment an hour later, Margaret and Dr Banks had a point. She no longer actively wanted to die. Killing herself would be a poor tribute to Richard and the life they'd had together. She had to go on living, make some kind of life for herself, make more of an effort, if for no other reason than that Margaret would then perhaps stop worrying about her.

She'd had the prescription filled on her way home and now dutifully went into the kitchen to wash down one of the gigantic brown capsules with water. And tomorrow morning, she promised herself, I'll start swimming.

CHAPTER TWO

PAULA hadn't been down to the Olympic-sized pool in the basement of the building since the manager had shown it to her when they first got the apartment two years ago. Richard had used it occasionally, but Paula had never been athletic.

She wasn't even quite sure how to get to it, she realised the next morning when she got off the elevator at the basement level and was immediately faced with a maze of corridors leading in three different directions. Since she had trouble sleeping anyway, she had decided the best time for her prescribed swim would be six o'clock in the morning. At that ungodly hour, she reasoned, she would most likely have the pool to herself.

Finally, she chose a corridor and was relieved to see a sign a short way down indicating the direction of the pool. It was eerily silent in the long narrow hallway, with only her footsteps echoing on the concrete floor and the distant hum of a generator or furnace.

She came to a heavy metal door, painted the same yellow as the solid brick walls, with a sign on it. Pool Area. She pulled it open and stepped into a damp cavernous room, well-heated, the light green water of the large pool shimmering under the dim lights set high on the ceiling.

She also saw that there was someone in the pool, a solitary figure swimming noiselessly up and down with slow, powerful strokes. Her heart sank. She had hoped to be alone. She stood hesitantly at a canvas chair on the wide concrete apron debating what to do.

It was a very large pool, she thought. The lone swimmer, obviously masculine, was close to one edge. If she swam along the opposite side from him there was no reason why she would even have to acknowledge his presence.

She slipped off her short white towelling robe and laid it over the chair, still not sure what she should do. If she left now and came back later, chances were there would be even more people.

Finally, she stepped out of her rubber-soled sandals and moved cautiously to the edge of the pool. She kept her eyes averted from the other swimmer on the principle that if she pretended he wasn't there he would ignore her, too.

She dipped one toe in the water. It was just the right temperature, not quite lukewarm. Still she hesitated. Then she heard a sudden splashing noise from the opposite side. Startled, she glanced over to see a tall, tanned masculine form heaving itself out of the water. Before she could turn away, their eyes met briefly and she was horrified to recognise Senator Matthew Stratton standing not twenty feet away from her.

A slow flush began to spread through her. She hadn't wanted to see anyone, much less someone she knew. Not only was she anxious to avoid conversation, but earlier she had been appalled at how the once snug two-piece bathing suit hung on her since she had lost so much weight.

'What—what are you doing here?' she blurted out at last. Had he followed her? she thought wildly. Had Margaret sent him?

Still panting slightly from exertion, he reached for a towel, ran it over his face and head briefly, then draped it around his neck.

'I live here,' he calmly replied. He took a step towards her, frowning, and she shrank back. Then she saw recognition dawning in the hard grey eyes. 'You're William Chandler's sister,' he said at last.

'Sister-in-law,' she corrected feebly. The sight of all that bare masculine flesh unsettled her.

He was a powerfully built man, long and lean, with a smooth, tanned chest. The water-soaked black bathing trunks hung low on his spare frame, clinging damply to his hips and thighs.

'Yes,' he said. 'Paula. The matchmaker's sister.' His eyes narrowed at her. 'You live here, too?'

All of a sudden it dawned on her that *he* was suspicious of *her*! It was almost funny. Damn Margaret and her machinations! How was she going to explain to this man that she had no designs on him?

'Yes. Of course I do,' she replied. 'I've lived here for two years.' Somehow she felt obliged to assert her right to be there.

'But you've only just begun to swim in the pool,' came the dry observation.

'I didn't think anyone would be here this early,' she explained tartly.

He gave her a curt nod and slowly began walking away from her towards the men's locker room. 'There isn't usually,' he said over his shoulder. 'That's why I come at this time.'

When he was gone, Paula stood for several moments at the edge of the pool trembling with anger and mortification at the man's rudeness. Who did he think he was? Did he automatically assume that every woman who came within a mile of him was out to trap him? A typical, arrogant male reaction, she thought bitterly. They all think they're God's gift to women.

She turned and dived into the water, more to cool her anger than anything else, and dutifully swam the ten lengths she had resolved upon. By the time she was through, she felt better. Matthew Stratton would be long gone by now, and as she dried herself and pulled on her robe, the whole affair had taken on a humorous aspect in her mind.

Later that morning, as she worked on her drawings, Paula thought over the strange early morning encounter. The more she thought about it, the funnier it seemed.

It was clear that the cold, withdrawn senator wanted to avoid emotional involvements as much as she did. At least with her, she added wryly. Then she remembered how he had held himself so aloof from the seductive Michele Lathrop at the dance after the reception for him two weeks ago.

She wondered idly what he was running from. Margaret had said he wasn't married. Well, what difference did it make? She'd simply swim at a different time. Noon, she decided, and have a late lunch. That way she wouldn't have to bump into Senator Matthew Stratton at all.

'Well, I must say,' Margaret commented, 'that I see a decided improvement in your looks.'

It was two weeks later, and Paula had stuck to her exercise and vitamins religiously. She had to admit that her appetite had improved, and she was sleeping the night through at last.

Margaret was arranging flowers, hothouse lilies and roses, in the large, gracefully proportioned living room of the Chandler home in Virginia in preparation for what she called a 'small intimate' dinner party. That was Margaret's euphemistic phrase for at least twenty people, and Paula had driven out from Washington early to help her, planning to spend the night.

'I'm feeling much better,' she responded now. 'Do you want to put out the cold canapés now, or shall we wait until the first guests arrive?'

'Oh, it's almost six,' Margaret said. 'Might as well set them down now.' She gave her sister an appraising look. 'What else did Dr Banks say?'

'Nothing. No dread diseases. Just that I was a little run down. He gave me some potent vitamins and told me to get more exercise.'

'And are you?' Margaret asked sharply. 'Exercising?'

Paula set down the silver tray of canapés on the low marble-topped table in front of the fireplace. 'Yes, sister dear, I'm swimming religiously every day. I go down at noon. It's not so crowded then.'

'Well, as I say, you do look better. You've even gained a little weight, although I must say that dress doesn't do much for you. For a fashion illustrator, you're not the best advertisement for your product.'

Paula glanced down at her black dress. It was two years old and still a little large for her. The dress itself was a heavy silk crepe with a round scooped neckline and little cap sleeves. She had camouflaged the loose fit with a short white satin jacket, heavily beaded with black paillettes.

'What's wrong with it?' she asked defensively.

'Oh, nothing,' Margaret retorted drily. 'Except that it doesn't fit you and. . .'

'Anybody home?' came a loud voice from the front hall, interrupting Margaret's carping monologue.

Thank God, Paula breathed to herself. William. She turned to greet her brother-in-law, but the smile on her face faded when she saw that Matthew Stratton was directly behind him, half a head taller, and staring at her now with knowing grey eyes that glinted with sudden, irritated comprehension.

Paula was so angry she could barely contain herself. She set her jaw in a firm line, clenched her fists at her sides and glared at her sister. Margaret met her glance briefly, then turned quickly away and walked towards the two men.

'Hello, darling,' she said to her husband, pecking him briefly on the cheek. 'And Senator Stratton. How nice that you came out with William. No sense bringing two cars. I hope you can spend the night. We have lots of room.'

Paula watched as the tall man's eyebrows lifted slightly. 'That was the understanding,' he murmured. He gave William a questioning look.

'Yes,' Margaret burbled on, 'and then you can drive back to Washington late tomorrow with Paula.' She gave her sister a bright smile. 'We can all spend the day together.'

Oh, no, Paula thought, as the pieces of Margaret's plan fell into place in her head. Not this time, sister dear. You've embarrassed me once too often with your matchmaking, and I've been too polite to resist. This time you can wriggle out of it yourself.

'I'm afraid not,' she said firmly. 'I'm driving back tonight.'

'Oh, but you can't,' Margaret protested.

'Yes I can,' Paula replied calmly.

There was an uncomfortable silence then, but Paula stood her ground. Margaret has bullied me for the last time, she vowed, and if her guest is offended, she can deal with it herself.

Then she heard Matthew Stratton's voice cut into the stillness. 'There's no problem,' he said smoothly. He turned to William, who stood red-faced beside him. 'You said something about an early morning meeting at the State Department. I'll just get up early and go along with you.'

'Well, uh, of course,' William said with forced heartiness. 'That'll be fine.' He shot his wife a hangdog look.

Margaret opened her mouth to protest, but Paula forestalled her. 'That's all settled, then,' she said with finality. 'I'll just go see to the rest of the canapés.'

Soon the other guests began trickling in, and by the time they were all gathered together over drinks in front of the roaring fire, it was clear to Paula that even Margaret had outdone herself in brass this time. There were only six other guests, three married couples who lived nearby. Paula knew them well. She and Matthew Stratton were the only unattached people there.

She did her best to avoid him throughout the cocktail hour without being actually rude to him, and was grateful to see that he was avoiding her as well. She did notice, glancing at him from time to time, that he was downing martinis at an alarming rate, but when they sat down to dinner at the long dining table, he seemed to be in complete control of himself. If anything, he was quieter and more withdrawn than she remembered him from their two previous encounters at the reception and the swimming pool.

Naturally, Paula thought wryly, as she spread her napkin on her lap, Margaret had seated them next to each other at dinner. Trust her sister to do the obvious. She couldn't continue to ignore him at such close quarters, she decided, but she could set him straight once and for all.

He was silent throughout dinner, eating little and steadily drinking wine. He answered politely when any of the other guests spoke to him, but seemed to be off in a world of his own, his voice automatic, expressionless.

Finally, when the others were involved in a heated discussion of the situation in the Middle East, always a hot topic at Washington parties, she turned to him and spoke.

'Senator Stratton.' He was staring off into space, ostensibly listening to the others' conversation, but from the blank expression in the steely eyes, Paula could see that his mind was miles away. 'Senator Stratton,' she repeated in a louder tone.

Slowly he turned to her and gradually focused the grey eyes on hers. 'Matthew,' he said. 'My name is Matthew.'

Was he drunk? Paula wondered. He seemed in control of himself. He was obviously a very controlled man in any case, and the amount of liquor he had consumed only seemed to emphasise the rather stern remote quality she had noticed in him before.

Keeping her voice low so that the others wouldn't hear, and leaning towards him slightly, she said, 'I want to apologise for my sister.'

The cold grey eyes looked directly into hers for a moment, and one dark eyebrow quirked up. 'Apologise?' He took a swallow of wine, draining his glass. 'What for? She's a superb hostess.'

A ghost of a smile hovered about the thin lips.

Why, Paula thought, he's laughing at me, amused by the whole thing. Anger rose up in her and she was about to make a sharp retort when she suddenly saw something in his eyes that was hauntingly familiar to her.

This man is in a great deal of pain, she realised, and she softened towards him, wondering what had put that look there and what it had to do with the amount of liquor he was consuming.

She smiled back at him. 'My apology was for the set-up tonight,' She waved her hand vaguely towards the others. Someone was shouting now, and she had to raise her voice to be heard. I'm afraid it's pretty obvious that Margaret chose you to be "it" for the evening.' His face went blank. 'I mean, my escort,' she went on to explain.

Comprehension dawned on the dark features. 'Oh, that,' he said, dismissing Margaret and her matchmaking airily. 'I'm used to that.'

'Well, I should be, too, I guess, since she's done it often enough at my expense, but it still bothers me.'

'Why?' he asked. 'Why should it bother you?'

She shrugged. 'It's embarrassing, for one thing. It puts me in an awkward position and the poor men she pounces on at a terrible disadvantage.'

He leaned back lazily in his chair and gave her a long look. 'I don't feel in the least at a disadvantage.'

No, she thought, this man obviously wouldn't feel at a disadvantage anywhere or under any circumstances. 'I'm glad,' she said weakly.

'Tell me,' he said slowly, choosing each word carefully, 'why does a situation like this make you feel awkward? Don't you want to meet unattached men?'

'No,' she said fervently. 'I don't. And Margaret knows it.'

At that moment, Margaret rose to her feet at the foot of the table and the imperious voice rang out. 'We'll have our coffee in the living room by the fire,' she announced, and her guests slowly began to move away from the table.

Paula saw very little of Matthew Stratton for the rest of the evening. She heard him answer politely when spoken to, but for the most part he seemed to be wrapped in a cloak of morose silence. She noticed too that he was rarely without a drink in his hand, and at one point in the party, he seemed to have vanished altogether.

Her curiosity was piqued. At the reception a month or so ago, he had been reserved but not totally withdrawn as he seemed to be this evening. It was as though he was on another planet.

Finally, just before midnight, Paula saw her chance to leave. Margaret was speaking to the other three women in the party and wouldn't be able to raise a fuss.

'I must be going, Margaret,' she said firmly, and before her sister could utter a word, Paula turned to the other women, said good night and walked away.

William followed her into the entry hall and helped her on with her coat. He was frowning when he turned to kiss her lightly on the forehead.

'I don't like your driving back to town by yourself so late at night.' There was a concerned look in the kind brown eyes.

'I'll be all right, William. It's only an hour's drive, and the security is good in my building.' She hesitated a moment, then plunged on. 'You'd be doing me an enormous favour, William,' she said in a low voice, 'if you could convince Margaret to give up this mania for marrying me off.'

He sighed. 'I know. She thinks she's doing it for your own good, Paula, but it's clear to me, at least, that you really mean what you say.'

'I really do, William.'

He nodded slowly. 'All right, then. I'll be firm with her.'

'Thank you,' she said, and stepped out on to the porch. 'Don't come with me, William. It's freezing out here. Good night.'

She smiled to herself as she walked out into the cold night air. William being firm with Margaret was like a mouse being firm with a lion. Paula could never understand how a man like William, who was a real power in government, could be so cowardly where his wife was concerned.

Paula pulled her heavy wool coat around her tightly as she walked the few yards to where her car was parked. It was not quite freezing out, but close, she thought. The night sky was clear, with no moon, but a million stars twinkled overhead and the air was fresh and invigorating.

As she approached the small red Corvette, partly illuminated by the front porch light, partly in the shadow of a large tree, she saw what looked like the shape of a man leaning against the side of the car.

She stopped in her tracks, fear clutching at her heart, and opened her mouth to call to William, who, she knew, was still standing by the front door waiting to see that she got safely into her car.

Then she heard a familiar low voice—'Will you please give me a lift back to town?'—and Matthew Stratton took a step towards her, out of the shadows and into the light.

The cry died on her lips. One look at the haggard face told her that this was no time to ask questions or argue. The firm jaw was set, lifted slightly, the dark eyes hooded. He had had too much to drink, she knew, but the ravaged look on his face came from a source far more significant than liquor.

She made up her mind in a flash and called to William. 'Matthew has changed his mind.' She was amazed to hear how clear and steady her voice sounded as it rang out in the dark night. 'He's going back to town with me.'

'All right, then.' She heard William's faintly puzzled reply and his retreating footsteps as he went inside and shut the door.

By the time Paula got into the driver's seat, Matthew was already inside the car. His long legs were spread out loosely in front of him, his dark head leaning back on the seat, his eyes closed.

Paula started the car and waited a moment while the engine warmed up. 'The others are going to wonder why you went off like this,' she said calmly. 'You know what Washington gossip is like. There will be talk.'

He opened one eye. 'Not half as much as if I'd shown up back in there in my condition.' He spoke slowly, enunciating each word precisely. There was finality in his strained voice, and the eye closed.

Those were the last words spoken between them for the remainder of the trip into town. Paula glanced over at him from time to time. He seemed to be asleep. He was drunk, she knew, but he didn't act like any drunk she'd ever encountered before. He seemed to be completely aware of his condition, even to the point of choosing the best way to handle it.

She thought of the way he had downed his drinks during the evening, almost as though he was cold-bloodedly setting out to pass into oblivion. Yet not once had she heard him slur his words or seen him stumble. He seemed to know the point he wanted to reach, got there deliberately, then stayed there.

She pulled off the interstate linking Virginia and Washington, and on to the beltway that encircled the capital. There was little traffic this time of night, and before long she had driven into the apartment garage and parked the Corvette in her space.

The garage was dimly lit, and when she turned to the man sleeping peacefully beside her, she took a closer look at him. With the cold grey eyes closed, the thin mouth relaxed, he didn't look nearly as forbidding as he had before, and it dawned on her suddenly that he was really quite a handsome man.

He had unbuttoned the top button of his white dress shirt and loosened the dark muted tie so that she could see the hollow at the base of his throat and the little pulse pounding there. His hair, usually combed neatly, was dishevelled, a black lock falling over his forehead.

Yet, in spite of the relaxed posture and peaceful expression on his face, she could still see the traces of pain in the deep lines around his eyes, across his forehead and cutting down from the straight nose to the corners of his mouth. What had put them there? She felt a strange impulse to reach out and smooth away those tell-tale, revealing lines, to draw him to her, to comfort him. No stranger to pain herself, she was intuitively empathetic to the sufferings of others.

Then he opened his eyes. He blinked and sat up straight, focusing now on Paula. He shook his head a little, as if to clear it, then leaned forward, his elbows resting on his knees, his head in his hands.

'Are you all right?' Paula asked in a low voice. 'Can you make it to your apartment by yourself?'

She surprised herself by her concern. Usually drunks only disgusted her, but some instinct told her that Matthew Stratton was no ordinary drunk, only a man in pain who had deliberately set out to allay it in the only way open to him.

He looked at her then, the grey eyes glazed. 'I-I'm sorry.' For the first time his voice faltered. 'If you could just help me to my door, I'd appreciate it. Don't want to pass out in the hall and create a scandal.'

'Of course,' she murmured.

He seemed to be fairly steady on his feet, as she took his arm and led him to the elevator. He told her he lived on the sixth floor, and they made it without mishap or running into anyone to the door of his apartment. He fumbled in his trousers pocket for his key and handed it to her. She unlocked the door and guided him inside.

'Would you like me to make you some coffee?' she asked.

They were standing just inside the door. It was quite dark, and Paula fumbled on the wall for the light switch, which didn't seem to be in the same spot as it was in her own apartment, three floors below.

Suddenly, she heard him give a low groan, felt him lurch towards her, and the next thing she knew, his arms had come around her, clasping her so tightly she could scarcely breathe. Automatically, she struggled, but she soon realised that there was nothing remotely erotic about the way he held her. It was more like a drowning man holding on to a life raft.

She put her arms up, then, around his neck, and ran her hands over the thick hair in a soothing comforting motion. They stood this way for several moments, clinging together, neither of them uttering a word.

Gradually, his hold on her relaxed. His hands slipped inside her coat and began to move on her body, warm and strong, first her waist, then up under her short jacket to her bare back, and she realised that the innocent embrace was turning into something far more sensual than she was prepared to handle.

She removed her hands from around his neck and put them up against his chest to push him away. He only pulled her closer, and his head came down, his mouth hard on hers.

For one split second, she softened, responded, but the moment she felt his tongue against her lips, forcing them open, she turned her head away so that his mouth was at her ear.

He was muttering now, hoarsely, incoherently. What was he saying? It was one word, over and over again. Paula strained to hear him. It was a name. 'Beth,' it came again. 'Beth.'

She knew she had to put a stop to this right away. It had already gone too far. The closeness to the hard male body, his harsh breath in her ear, his hands still moving up and down her back were beginning to set her own pulses racing. It did no good to struggle or try to pull away. It only made him strengthen that iron grip.

Then, she felt his hand move around and clutch

at her breast. She gasped aloud at the touch. He was tugging now at the low, loose bodice, the large hand warm and possessive on her bare skin, and she knew that one second more and it would be too late to stop him—or herself. She pulled herself together with an effort and reached out again to try to find the light switch. This time she was successful. She flicked it on, and the room was immediately bathed in light.

'Matthew,' she said in a loud, clear voice. 'It's Paula. Do you hear me? Do you understand? I'm not Beth, I'm Paula.'

Instantly, the hand stilled on her breast, then dropped away. He stood motionless for a moment, his head bent, then drew slowly back from her, looking down at her with a dazed expression. Gradually, recognition dawned in his eyes, and with it came the pain.

She couldn't bear it. Her own memories came flooding back, memories that simmered constantly just below the surface of her life. God, she thought, as she covered her face with her hands, would it never end?

With a little cry, she pulled open the door and ran out into the corridor. She flew to the elevator, praying he wouldn't follow her, not daring to look back, and when it came she darted inside and slumped against the wall. She punched the button for her floor, and only then, as the doors began to slide closed, did she dare to look down the hall. It was empty.

The next day was Saturday. Paula had been given a commission from one of the leading dress shops in Washington to illustrate several outfits in their new spring line for *Harpers Bazaar*. If she didn't get started on them soon, she wouldn't meet the deadline.

Although Richard's insurance had left her well-provided with the necessities of life, and they had owned the apartment outright, the extra money she earned from her illustrating work helped her just over the edge of genteel poverty and gave her a sense of independence, even a commitment of sorts. At least her work provided some direction in her otherwise empty life.

She enjoyed her work. Well aware that her minor talent for drawing would never lead to the creation of great art, still she knew she was good within her limited sphere of endeavour.

As she settled down at her work table, she thought about Matthew Stratton and his strange behaviour last night. In the cold light of day it seemed almost like a dream. Had he really held her? Kissed her? The shape he was in, he was hardly accountable for his actions, she decided, and probably wouldn't even remember that short, highly charged moment between them.

What would she say to him, she wondered, if they met again? They could hardly hope to avoid each other, living in the same building, travelling in the same social circles. She finally decided that the wisest course would be to put the whole thing out of her mind, pretend it had never happened, and concentrate on her work.

It was odd, she thought now as she sketched in the outlines of a luscious sapphire-blue linen suit on her drawing pad, that she should have this talent for fashion illustrating when she really possessed very little clothes sense. She only copied what she saw before her on the dress form she used to hang the clothes on.

Too thin, now, since Richard's death, she had always been slim, with a model's figure, elegant rather than voluptuous, with small firm breasts, slim hips and waist and a flat stomach. Although she was tall, her bone structure was small and delicate, so that whatever she wore seemed to hang well on her.

She was grateful, too, for the generous discounts she received on the clothes she drew for the various stores in town. It really didn't matter much to her any more what she wore, but she did need clothes, and at least this way she didn't have to shop for them.

There had been frost on the small patch of lawn in front of the building that morning, as she had expected there would be last night. The sun shone palely through the windows across the front of the living room. A small fire was burning in the grate, and there was a steaming cup of coffee on the table beside her.

She had been working steadily for over an hour when the doorbell rang, disturbing her concentration. Frowning at the interruption, she glanced at her watch. Eleven o'clock, she saw with some surprise, almost time to stop anyway. She dropped her pencil, flexed her cramped fingers and went to the door.

When she opened it and saw Matthew Stratton standing there, a warm flush of embarrassment stole through her whole body. Not only did she look a wreck, she thought, running a hand through her short dark hair, but she thought she had convinced herself that last night's episode would be the end of their dealings with each other.

'Good morning,' she managed to say at last.

'May I come in?' he asked in a low subdued voice.

She hesitated and looked at him, suddenly unsure of herself. He was dressed casually in dark trousers, a white shirt open at the neck and a charcoal grey pullover. His face was drawn, the silvery eyes slightly bloodshot, but his flat cheeks and chin were freshly shaven and his thick dark hair neatly combed.

'You've caught me at a bad time,' she said at last with a vague gesture towards her work table. 'I'm working.'

'This will only take a few minutes.' His voice was determined, almost grim, and she suddenly realised that he was very uncomfortable himself, as though he had set himself a distasteful task and was forcing himself to go through with it.

She nodded, then, and opened the door a little wider, gesturing for him to step inside. When she had closed the door behind him, she glanced up at him and saw his eyes flick briefly around the comfortable living room, at the cheery fire burning in the grate, the warm gold and rust tones of the carpet and upholstery. They finally lit on the dress form with the blue suit hanging there, and he turned to her with raised eyebrows.

She spread her hands wide and smiled. 'My work,' she explained. 'I'm a fashion illustrator.'

'I see.' He frowned then, looking down at his feet, as though he was having trouble getting started.

'Would you like some coffee?' she asked briskly.

He nodded, obviously relieved. 'Thank you, I would.' A faint rueful smile hovered over the firm lines of his mouth. 'I've already drunk gallons. It seems to help.'

'Sit down, then. I'll get the pot.'

As she went into the kitchen to get a clean mug

and the pot of coffee, she wondered how much he remembered about last night. She hoped fervently that he had forgotten the part about calling her Beth, kissing her, holding her, caressing her. If he didn't recall it, she reasoned, it wouldn't be so bad.

When she came back, she sat down beside him on the long rust-coloured sofa and set the coffee things down on the low table in front of them. She poured him a cup, handed it to him, and after a few swallows, he began to speak.

'I came to apologise to you for last night,' he said in a stiff tone. 'I can't remember all of what happened,' he continued drily, 'but what I do recall is bad enough.'

He turned the grey eyes on her in a direct piercing gaze. Odd, Paula thought, looking away, he seems sincere, but there wasn't a hint of humble supplication in his tone.

'It's all right,' she murmured into her cup. 'Nothing very terrible happened. You had a little too much to drink. I gave you a ride home, helped you find your apartment, and that was it.' She looked at him, then, and saw relief flooding into his face. 'After all,' she added lightly, 'what are neighbours for?'

'You're very kind,' he murmured. 'I don't ordinarily do that sort of thing.'

'You handled it very well, I thought. I doubt if the others knew just how far gone you were.' She laughed. 'The drunks I've known are usually quite obnoxious, and start shouting and slobbering after a while. You just got quieter.'

'Well, that's a relief.' He gave her another wintry smile. 'I woke up this morning with the vague recollection—aside from a hell of a hangover—that I had done something unforgivable, but I couldn't for the life of me remember what it was.'

'No,' she said cheerfully, fibbing just a little. Then she added, 'Your public image is still safe.'

He shot her a dark look. 'I wasn't talking about that,' he said curtly. 'I was talking about you.' He shook his head. 'I can't get rid of the idea that I somehow...' He paused, then shrugged his shoulders and plunged on. 'That I somehow forced myself on you.'

A dark red flush stole across Paula's face at his words. He had remembered! Carefully, she set her cup down on the coffee table, averting her face.

'It was nothing,' she murmured.

'But it was something,' he shot back immediately. 'Please tell me. I don't want to embarrass you, but I've got to know.'

She drew in a deep breath and turned to him. Now she did see something like supplication in his eyes and that old haunting pain. She decided then to be honest with him. Matthew Stratton was no mere drunken playboy, but a serious man with a weight of some kind on his heart that perhaps she could lighten by telling him the truth.

She lifted her chin. 'All right, then. You kissed me.' She hesitated. 'And you called me Beth.' When she saw the look of pain on his face deepen, she instantly regretted her words. She put a hand out towards him, not quite touching him. 'I'm sorry. Really, it was nothing. I understood. Please just forget about it. I have.'

He stood up then and crossed over to a window in long strides. Lifting aside the curtain, he stood staring out into the street below.

'I thought it must have been something like that,' he ground out finally. He turned, then, and stood there facing her, his hands shoved in his trouser pockets, the dark head bent. He began speaking in a low monotone.

'I don't want to make you any more uncomfortable than I already have, but I feel I really must explain my actions to you. I don't want you to think. . .' His voice trailed off and he spread his hands in a gesture of helplessness.

'Beth was my wife,' he went on. 'She died two years ago yesterday.' He ran a hand over his hair. 'It was the anniversary of her death.'

Paula was stunned. She felt the tears begin to gather, stinging her eyes, as her own painful memories flooded back into her mind. She gave him one stricken look, then covered her face with her hands, unable to staunch the sudden torrent, and began to sob brokenly.

She dimly heard Matthew cross the room, felt his weight as he settled next to her on the sofa, sensed his presence next to her, not touching, not speaking, but somehow comforting just by being there.

Finally, it was over. She reached in the pocket of her jeans and pulled out a handkerchief, wiped her eyes, blew her nose and turned to him with a weak smile. His expression was grave, contrite.

'Sorry,' she said. 'It just all came back suddenly. I've never done that before, at least not in front of anyone else. I'm sorry it had to be you.'

'You, too, then?' he asked softly.

She sighed and blew her nose again. 'Yes. Not quite a year ago. A boating accident.' She gave him a stark, dismal look. 'Does it never end?'

He looked away. 'They say it does,' he said bleakly. 'Eventually. I wouldn't know.'

'It hasn't for you, though,' she said flatly,

making it a statement rather than a question. He shook his head. 'Nor for me,' she went on. 'It never will.'

He looked at her than. 'No,' he said. He got to his feet. 'Well, it looks as though I've done more harm with my apology than good.' His voice was brisk. 'I'd better go before I do any more damage.'

She walked with him to the door, the odd realisation stealing over her that she felt better than she had in a long time. At the door they stood for a moment facing each other.

'No,' she said shyly. 'You didn't do any damage. It was good for me to let go like that. Other people—my sister, for example—mean well, but unless you've gone through a terrible loss like that yourself, you can't possibly understand.'

He smiled briefly. 'That's all right, then.' He paused, then said, 'I also wanted to apologise for my rudeness at the swimming pool a few weeks ago. I like to swim alone, and when I saw you, I thought. . .'

'I know what you thought,' she interrupted drily. 'Margaret and her matchmaking again.'

He smiled briefly and nodded. 'Something like that,' he admitted.

'I hope you realise now that you have nothing to fear from me,' she went on in the same dry tone.

'I was never afraid of you.' There was a short silence. 'You haven't been back.'

'No. I'm swimming later. It's practically empty at noon, and now that I'm sleeping better, I'm not up quite so early.'

'What's your secret?' he asked. 'For sleeping better.'

The haggard look was back, and she felt a sudden rush of sympathy for him. She knew instinctively he would resent pity, however, and replied lightly, 'Oh, vitamins, exercise, and a tyrannical sister. She does have her uses, you know.'

When he was gone, Paula leaned back against the door and closed her eyes. For the first time in months she could think of Richard without that terrible sense of dread despair. She missed him. She would always miss him, always love him. No one could ever take his place in her heart, but her breakdown today in front of Matthew had worked a kind of catharsis in her.

She was grateful for that, she thought, as she cleared away the coffee things, but she knew she didn't want it to happen again. What's more, she had the strong conviction that he felt the same way, and that he would be no more anxious to see her than she would be to see him.

CHAPTER THREE

IN the month that followed, however, they did see each other often. It was hardly to be avoided, but it was almost always at a distance, across the room at a large gathering. When this happened, they would nod and smile at each other, but neither made any effort to seek the other out. Once they sat at the same table at a dinner party in a restaurant. They spoke politely when it was unavoidable, but only on the most impersonal subjects.

He was always paired with a blonde, and Paula thought wryly that the word from Baltimore must have got round to Washington hostesses. Somehow, though, he never seemed to be *with* the blonde of the evening, no matter how inviting or beautiful she might be. Even the devastating Michele didn't seem able to penetrate that cold reserve, that remote shell.

With her new health regime, Paula found that she was feeling better all the time. Even the indomitable Margaret seemed satisfied with her progress. She still managed to come up with suitable escorts for her besides David Wyatt, but appeared to be finally resigned to the fact that when Paula said she was not interested in romance, she really meant it.

She spent Christmas with William and Margaret. Their two children were home from school for the holidays, and with snow on the ground, gifts under the tree and a sumptuous turkey dinner, the day passed pleasantly enough. Still, Paula was glad to get back to the quiet of her own apartment.

In early January she managed to get through the first anniversary of Richard's death. Although the weight on her heart was heavier that day than usual, when it was over, she felt as though she had passed an important milestone, and the tears she shed that night when she gazed longingly at his photograph on the bedside table before turning out the light were not bitter.

During Christmas week, the city had been virtually deserted as all the government officials fled Washington for their own family homes. Now, however, the tempo would pick up again, and Paula braced herself for a new round of social activities.

On a Wednesday night in late January she decided to attend a concert at the Kennedy Center where a young Korean cellist she particularly wanted to hear was playing. Margaret, who preferred more active pursuits than sitting in a darkened theatre listening to music, had offered Paula her own seat in the Chandler box, while she herself was off at yet another tedious reception.

As she locked the door of her apartment and walked down the hall to the elevator, Paula thought how grateful she was that this was one affair, at least, where Margaret agreed with her that she didn't need an escort. There was room for ten people in the box, and no need to pair off.

She wondered, waiting for the elevator, if she should drive or take a cab. It had been raining steadily for days, with no sign of freezing, so perhaps it would be safe to take her own car. On the other hand, parking near the busy Center was at a premium.

Still absorbed in her inner debate, when the elevator doors opened she was dimly aware that there was another passenger inside. Then she heard a familiar voice say good evening to her. She jumped a little, then looked up into the amused grey eyes of Matthew Stratton.

She hadn't seen him for some weeks, and was surprised now at how tall he seemed. He was wearing a trench coat, unbelted, over a dark suit, and looked tanned and fit, as though he'd been in the sun over the holidays.

'You look as though you're pondering a weighty matter,' he said as she stepped inside.

She laughed. 'Oh, I was. I'm trying to decide whether to take a cab to the Kennedy Center or drive. What's your opinion?'

'Don't tell me,' he said. 'William's box?'

She stared at him. 'Oh, no,' she groaned. 'You too?' He nodded gravely.

'*Damn* Margaret!' she muttered. 'I thought she'd given that up.'

He smiled. The elevator had reached the ground floor, and they stepped out into the lobby and faced each other.

'I take it she didn't provide you with an escort for the evening?' he asked. 'Odd, I was invited alone, too.'

Paula almost gnashed her teeth she was so angry. 'One of these days,' she ground out, 'I'm going to murder that sister of mine.'

'You could be wrong, you know,' he said musingly. 'William gave me my ticket. He knows I like music. It could just be coincidence.'

She glared up at him. 'Do you really believe that?'

He shrugged. 'It's possible.'

She began to turn her anger on him. He seemed to be amused at the awkward situation. 'Well, I

just won't go,' she announced. She turned to
punch the elevator button.

'Oh, come on. What's the harm?' he asked
lightly. 'Are you ashamed to be seen with me?'

'Of course not,' she replied hotly. 'It's not that.'

'Actually, I'm probably a lot safer than young
Wyatt or the other charming young men your sister
provides.'

'You make her sound like an escort bureau,'
Paula said, beginning to see the humour of the
situation.

'Well?'

She laughed. The elevator door opened and she
started to step inside. 'I'm still not going,' she said
firmly. 'It's time—long past time—to put my foot
down. I'm tired of being manipulated.' She gave
him a defiant look. 'Besides, I can find my own
escorts.'

'I'm sure you can,' he agreed. He had put his
shoulder up against the elevator door to hold it
open. 'Come on. Be a sport. Don't you like music?'

'Well, yes, of course I do. Why else would I go
out on a night like this?' She debated within
herself, tempted, but still angry.

'They're playing the second Haydn cello concerto,' he said gravely.

She looked up at him. He seemed to want her to
go, and at least it would solve her transportation
problem.

'Oh, all right then,' she said ungraciously and
stepped out of the elevator once again. 'I just hate
to give Margaret the satisfaction.'

'You could be wrong, you know,' he said as he
guided her towards his car. 'It really could be a
coincidence. At least give her the benefit of the
doubt.'

Seated on the long padded bench in front
mirrored wall at one end of the powder r
noticed as she gazed at her refle
overbright her eyes were. Probably fr
she thought, patting a light coatin
the skin around them.

She felt a fool for letting
sentimental tears. Yet he
understand the enormo
move her. Richard ha
tone deaf, and alway
him the orchestra

She stood up
She did loo
months ag
moire, a
the gr
she
lo

Then she felt Matthew leaning towards her,
nudging her gently with his arm. She looked down.
There was a neatly folded white handkerchief in
his hand. With a rueful smile and an apologetic
shrug, she took it from him and wiped her eyes.

At the intermission, they stood up and walked
out into the lobby to stretch their legs.

'Would you like a drink?' he asked, indicating
the bar set up at one end.

'Yes, please. I'll just slip into the Ladies to
repair the ravages of the Haydn.'

'Don't bother,' he said. 'You look fine. They
were honest tears.'

'Nevertheless,' she insisted with a smile, and
slipped away into the crowd.

of the
oom, she
ction how
om the tears,
g of powder on

Matthew observe her
seemed to instinctively
ds power music had to
made an effort, but was
ys claimed at concerts that to
never finished tuning up.
and smoothed her dress into place.
much better than she had two
o, she decided. The gown was a stiff
shimmering emerald colour that enhanced
en of her eyes. It had a square neckline, and
was gratified to see that her collar bones no
nger stuck out quite so sharply and that her
breasts now filled the bodice quite adequately.

She spotted Matthew standing at the busy bar at
the far end of the long lobby. There were two
glasses of champagne at his elbow and he was
glancing through the programme. As she watched
him, she felt a little tingle of pleasure at the
thought that this tall man, so handsome with his
tanned face against the brilliant white shirt, was
her escort.

Not that I have any personal interest in him, she
added quickly to herself as she began to walk
towards him. It was just that he was easy to be
with. She felt safe with him. He never gave off any
signs of the chase that she had had so much
trouble dealing with in other men, no sly
innuendoes, no unnecessary body contact, no deep
meaningful looks.

Still, she thought, she liked the way the silvery eyes lit up when he caught sight of her. Why had she ever thought he was cold? She remembered how he had given her his handkerchief during the Haydn, silently, without a word, seeming to understand exactly what she was feeling.

He handed her a glass and pointed to the programme in his hand. 'Have you read the second half of the concert?'

His tone was casual, unreadable. She took the programme from him and glanced over it as she sipped her champagne.

She tried to control the look of dismay that crossed her face when she finally looked up at him. 'Bartók?' she said weakly.

He grimaced. 'Bartók.' He raised an eyebrow. 'What do you think?'

Her mouth twitched. 'Honestly?'

'Honestly.' She could see that he was barely able to contain his own mirth.

She shook her head. 'Well, then, I detest Bartók.'

'Good,' he said flatly. He drained his glass. 'Are you hungry? I know a place that specialises in chocolate desserts. Once in a blue moon I indulge myself. How about it?'

She sighed. 'You've hit on my secret vice. I'm a confirmed chocoholic.'

'Drink up, then, and we'll get out of here. After the Haydn, I don't even want to hear the first note.'

They found a table at the little chocolate shop and ordered dessert and coffee. Paula chose a wickedly rich chocolate gateau, Matthew a creamy chocolate mousse.

'I could get drunk just on the *smell* in here,' Paula announced groaning. 'You've corrupted me. I never knew the place existed, and I've lived here all my life.'

He was leaning back in his chair, a cup of the thick rich coffee in front of him, a contented smile on his face.

'You'll have to practice restraint,' he said as he scraped the last bit of mousse from the glass bowl. 'I don't allow myself to even walk down this street very often.'

'You probably have more willpower than I do,' she sighed, and licked a crumb of the gateau off her upper lip.

He lit a cigarette and they sat in companionable silence while they drank their coffee, both satiated with the rich desserts.

'You look as though you've been in the sun,' Paula commented after a while.

'Yes. My parents spend their winters in Florida, Palm Beach, so the family usually gather together down there for the holidays.'

'That sounds great to me,' Paula said with a sigh. 'I hate the cold. It snowed here on Christmas day.'

He shrugged. 'The warm weather was nice, swimming in the surf, lying out in the sun. Florida beaches are hard to beat. Still, it's difficult to work up much Christmas spirit in eighty-degree weather surrounded by palm trees and oleander.'

She laughed. 'I suppose so, but I wouldn't mind giving it a try.' She paused. She didn't want to get personal, but she was curious. 'You mentioned your family,' she said tentatively, ready to drop the subject if he withdrew.

'Yes. I have a married older brother who runs

the family place in Maryland up near Hagerstown. Raises thoroughbred racehorses, apples—and one child.'

'That sounds wonderful,' she said. 'You grew up there?' He nodded. 'I envy you. I've always lived in the city. My father was in government service, too. It seems to run in the family. At least, Margaret and I both married into it.'

He hesitated for a moment, snubbed out his cigarette, then put his elbows on the table and leaned slightly towards her. 'Your husband, too?' His voice was cautious, casual, and she realized that he was giving her the same opportunity to back off the subject as she had given him a few minutes ago.

'Yes,' she said evenly, meeting his eyes. 'Richard worked with William in the Justice Department. That's how we met.'

He nodded briefly, then asked in a low tone, 'How is it? Any better?'

She nodded, knowing instinctively what he was referring to. 'Yes, it is.' She lifted her chin. 'I even got through the first anniversary of his death without going completely to pieces.'

He frowned. 'Then you did better than I did even after two years.' He shook his dark head disgustedly.

'Everyone handles grief in their own way, Matthew,' she said softly. 'With me it's tears, not eating properly, giving up. With you, it's a yearly drunk.'

He shot her a grateful look. 'I'm glad you realise it is only an annual event. With luck, it won't even be that eventually.' Then he lowered his voice and said, 'I've thought about calling you several times since, or speaking to you when we've met, to thank you again for being so understanding that night—and for helping me out of a sticky situation, keeping it quiet—but, I was afraid. . .' His voice trailed off.

She understood perfectly. 'Afraid I'd take it as a sign of personal interest?' He nodded glumly. She smiled. 'Matthew, I hope you realise by now that in spite of my sister's manoeuvres, I'm probably the last woman in Washington you have to worry about in that way.'

He leaned back, then, and gave her a long penetrating look. She flushed under his gaze. Had she offended him? Bruised his male ego? She hoped not. She suddenly realised how much she liked him, how comfortable she felt with him.

Finally he spoke. 'Yes,' he said. 'I do realise that.' He glanced down at his watch. 'It's getting late. Shall we go?'

Lying in bed that night, Paula wondered again if she had offended Matthew with her candour. He had been silent on the drive home, and seemed deep in thought, preoccupied, withdrawn. Yet, when he got off the elevator with her at her floor, walked with her to her apartment and saw her safely inside, he had smiled at her and thanked her for a pleasant evening.

She rolled over on to her stomach, hearing once again in her mind the gentle strains of the Haydn concerto, and as she drifted off to sleep, her last thought was of Matthew Stratton and how much she hoped she hadn't spoiled their budding friendship with her blunt honesty.

Next morning the telephone rang just as Paula was finishing breakfast. It was Margaret, and Paula flinched at the note of triumph in her sister's voice.

'I hear you were with Matthew Stratton at the concert last night,' she crowed.

Paula sighed. Really, the Washington grapevine moved at the speed of light. She took a deep breath, determined to set Margaret straight, right now. 'I wasn't *with* him, Margaret. He only gave me a lift. We met in the elevator and found we were both going to the same place. . .' She broke off. 'By the way, sister dear, was that one of your little plots to throw us together?'

'I swear, Paula, I had nothing to do with it. Honestly. I didn't even know William had given him the ticket. It was sheer coincidence. I've learned my lesson.'

Fat chance of that, Paula thought, but something in Margaret's voice rang true. She *never* backed down when faced with a valid accusation—she only became more aggressive—and was too self-assured to lie.

'I'm glad to hear it,' Paula said, mollified. 'It's about time.'

There was a short pause. Paula could practically hear Margaret panting at the other end of the line.

'Well?' her sister said at last. 'Aren't you going to tell me about it?'

'There's nothing to tell, Margaret. He gave me a lift. That's all there was to it.'

'Oh, come on, now. Beryl Armitage told me you disappeared together at the intermission. She said. . .'

'We both happen to detest Bartók and decided to leave early,' Paula interrupted firmly. 'That's all there was to it. Now, it's late. I have to get to work.'

'Work, work, work,' Margaret grumbled. 'That's all you ever think of.'

'You would, too, if your livelihood depended on it,' Paula countered lightly. 'I'll talk to you later.'

After she hung up the phone, she went into the bathroom to shower, cursing Beryl Armitage and the whole city's network that beat the FBI for gathering information.

She had just finished drying herself when the telephone rang again. Slipping on a robe she went back into the living room and lifted up the receiver.

'Mrs Waring?' came a brisk, feminine voice.

'Yes. This is she.'

'Senator Stratton's office. One moment please.'

There was a short silence, clicks, then Matthew's voice came on the line. 'Paula? It's Matthew.'

'Yes, Matthew.' She sat down on the edge of the chair in front of the desk, wondering why on earth he was calling her so early.

'Would it be possible for you to come into town to have lunch with me today?' he asked easily.

Her mind raced. What did he want? She was strongly tempted to refuse. Not only was she wary of masculine overtures, but she didn't want to feed the Washington gossip mill. Then she realised she was being paranoid. She liked the man, wanted his friendship, and she was almost certain that was all he wanted, too. Mature grown men and women could certainly have platonic friendships. Couldn't they?

'Paula?' came the curt voice. 'Are you there?'

'Yes, Matthew. Sorry. I was just thinking. Yes, I'd like to have lunch with you.'

'Good. How about one o'clock in the Senate Dining Room?'

'That would be fine.'

'See you then,' he said, and hung up.

CHAPTER FOUR

By the time they had had a drink and finished lunch, the Senate Dining Room was virtually empty. At a table across the room three solemn-faced men were deep in conversation, and at two or three other tables couples still sat lingering over a late lunch. The waiters had all disappeared.

Paula and Matthew sat at a table near a window overlooking the Capitol grounds, the great impressive dome dominating the surrounding area. During lunch they had chatted pleasantly about the concert last night, Paula's work and Matthew's position on various political issues, all on an impersonal, courteous plane.

He was good company, Paula thought now watching him as he leaned back and lit a cigarette. Ordinarily she found politics boring, but Matthew brought a personal note into the discussion that made it come alive for her. Also, he knew how to listen. He really paid attention to her when she spoke of her own work and never made it sound trivial or merely an idle feminine pastime.

They had been silent now for some moments, finishing up their coffee, and Paula had the odd feeling that he was studying her, debating within himself. She began to wonder if there wasn't more to the unexpected luncheon invitation than a mere social courtesy.

Finally, he seemed to make up his mind about something. He ground out his cigarette and leaned slightly towards her, his elbows on the table, his expression grave.

'You may have wondered why I asked you to come today,' he began slowly.

'A little,' she admitted, meeting the steady grey gaze.

'I have a proposition for you,' he said, watching her carefully. She couldn't hide the sudden look of alarm that flitted across her face, and he held up a hand, frowning slightly. 'Not that kind of proposition,' he said.

Paula clutched her handbag in her lap and waited. What could he be leading up to?

He exhaled deeply and leaned back in his chair. 'You and I don't know each other very well,' he went on in a serious tone, 'but in our brief acquaintance I've come to believe that we have one important thing in common.' He paused.

'Go on,' she said after a moment. 'What's that?'

His mouth quirked in a wry smile. 'Let's say we're both—emotionally adrift.' He shook his head. 'I don't quite know how to put it.'

'You're doing fine so far,' she said evenly, wondering what was coming.

'All right, then, to put it bluntly, I get the impression that you're as tired of, shall we say, importunate escorts, as I am of. : .' He broke off.

She smiled. 'Of possessive women?' she finished for him.

He nodded. 'You could put it that way,' he said drily.

Paula relaxed visibly. She looked down at the table and began toying idly with her fork. 'You're right,' she said with a sigh. 'At least you don't have Margaret pushing them at you.'

'No, but there are plenty of substitutes only too

eager to fill that function for me. Sometimes I wonder if romance is all middle-aged matrons have on their mind.'

'It's high on their list of priorities, at any rate,' she said with a little laugh. 'Well, then, what's your proposition? Shall we join forces and take out an advertisement in the *Washington Post*? I can see it now: "Mrs Paula Waring and Senator Matthew Stratton hereby respectfully request all matchmakers and marriage brokers to back off." Is that what you have in mind?'

He smiled with obvious amusement. 'Nothing quite that drastic, but I do suggest we join forces.' He sobered. 'Tell me, honestly, Paula, do you think you'll ever fall in love again? Want to marry again?'

Immediately, without even having to consider, she shook her head slowly from side to side. 'No. Never.'

'Never is a long time,' he said softly. 'You're still a young woman. A very attractive woman,' he added as an afterthought.

She frowned, trying to think of the words that would make him understand. 'I can only act on what I believe now.' She looked away. 'Richard was everything to me,' she said, struggling to keep the tremor out of her voice. 'The world, the sun, the moon, the stars. When he died, a part of me died with him. Every other man I've met is only a pale shadow of Richard.' She gave him an apologetic look. 'I'm sorry. But you of all people should understand what I mean.'

He held up a hand. 'Oh, I do,' he said. 'You don't have to worry about bruising my ego. I understand completely. Beth and I were childhood sweethearts. Her family had the farm next to ours.

Our mothers were best friends. It was always Beth, only Beth, for me.' He gazed out the window. 'I think I feel that by shutting out other women, I somehow keep her alive.'

'How did she die?' Paula asked softly.

'Cancer,' was the curt reply. 'Almost six months to the day after it was first diagnosed, she was gone.' The old haunting pain flickered briefly over his face, mingled now with anger and frustration. Then, recovering himself, he turned to her and forced a smile. 'It all happened so fast I guess I'm still reeling from it, two years later. I'm sorry.'

'I know the feeling,' Paula said. 'Please don't apologise.'

'Well,' he said in a brisk tone, 'it seems we understand each other quite well. What do you think of my proposition?'

'I'm not sure I quite grasp what you're driving at.'

'As I said, merely that we join forces. Neither of us can just drop out of Washington society. Between my position as a member of the Senate and your family, we're caught. It's probably healthier that way, anyway. You need an escort. I need someone to escort. We could let it be known—or assumed—that we have an exclusive relationship, and the pressure is off both of us.'

Paula still looked dubious. There were pitfalls to such a scheme, she knew, but right now she couldn't think of what they might be. And just what kind of relationship did he have in mind?

As if he could read her mind, he went on to explain hastily, 'Of course, the relationship would be purely platonic.'

'Of course,' she murmured, relieved. She thought it over for a few moments.

It just might work, she thought. The mere prospect of getting Margaret off her back was enough to convince her to give it a try, anyway. She looked at Matthew. He had lit another cigarette and sat calmly smoking, giving her time, not pressuring her. It was clear he had no ulterior motive. She wouldn't have to beat him off every time they were together.

'All right,' she said at last. 'Why not?'

'Fine.' He seemed pleased. He reached for the bill the waiter had left on the table and signed it. 'Perhaps we could start tonight. Beryl Armitage has invited me to a charity ball at the Mayflower Hotel.' His eyes flicked up at her. 'Did you receive an invitation?'

'Yes, but I declined. Beryl had it all arranged for me to go with her nephew. He's something in the Defense Department.' She grimaced. 'I've been out with him before. He's got ten hands and thinks every woman he meets is panting after him.'

He smiled, and Paula noticed once again that his smile never reached his eyes. 'Beryl asked me to give Michele Lathrop a lift,' he said wryly. 'I told her I wasn't sure when I'd be able to get away. You see, we've solved both our problems at one blow.' He stood up. 'Shall we go?'

He walked out to the car park with her, and when she had started the engine of the red Corvette, he leaned down to speak to her through the open window. 'I'll pick you up at eight. It's formal, if you recall. We'll make a grand debut.'

Paula experienced something like stage fright when she entered the grand ballroom of the Mayflower Hotel that night on the arm of the tall, impressive-looking senator. Their arrival together seemed uncomfortably like a deliberate deception to her, especially when they had both already declined invitations from other people.

She had dressed carefully that evening, just as though she were preparing for an appearance on the stage. At the last minute, she had almost backed out. The idea that had seemed so plausible when Matthew suggested it to her that afternoon now seemed ridiculous, even, she thought, a little dangerous.

Then he had appeared at her door, tall and solid, quietly self-assured, and she had to admit, breathtakingly attractive in his formal black suit and tie. Her qualms vanished. It just might work.

He had complimented her briefly, gravely, on the appearance she had laboured so diligently to achieve, and she couldn't help feeling a little let down at his distant tone. Her red velveteen dress fit her to perfection now that she had gained her weight back, and the colour, she knew, was just right for her delicate complexion and dark hair.

There hadn't been a trace of a gleam in the grey eyes when he first saw her. He seemed to be looking her over as he would one of the thoroughbred horses on his family's farm in Maryland. And when he held her coat for her as they were leaving her apartment, the long cool fingers that brushed her bare shoulders didn't linger a second more than was necessary.

She knew she was just being perverse to feel annoyed. Vain, she thought, as they drove the short distance from Georgetown to the hotel. She had become so accustomed to beating off male overtures that this aloof man's obvious lack of desire made her feel dowdy and unattractive.

At the door, Matthew had given his name to the

attendant and been told that they were to be seated at table twelve. They were one of the last to arrive, and by now the great ballroom was crowded with people. An orchestra was playing a slow tune, and there were several couples on the floor, dancing.

Each table surrounding the dance floor had a placard with a number on it, and as they threaded their way around the tables looking for number twelve, Paula was uncomfortably aware that several pairs of eyes were fastened on them. She spoke briefly to a few people she was acquainted with, and couldn't miss the avid looks of speculation as glances darted first on herself, then the tall man behind her, one hand lightly holding her by the elbow.

They spotted their table at last, and the first person Paula saw sitting there all alone was her sister, Margaret. She stiffened and started to turn, but the hand on her elbow tightened, propelling her gently forward.

Then she heard his voice in her ear, felt his breath on her cheek. 'Might as well get the worst over right away,' he murmured.

She knew immediately that he had planned it this way, had probably called Beryl Armitage and requested to be seated at the same table with William and Margaret. She fought down a moment of panic as she saw Margaret's eyes widen slowly in recognition, but when her mouth fell open, and Paula saw her sister speechless for once, she decided the whole scheme had been worth it.

With her head held high, she marched slowly forward and sat down next to her sister. Matthew had taken her coat, and after a brief greeting to the paralysed Margaret, went off to check it.

'Hello, Margaret,' Paula said blandly. She gazed around the room. 'There's quite a crowd here tonight. Beryl must have invited everyone in. . .'

'What are you doing here with Matthew Stratton?' Margaret cut in, finding her voice at last.

Paula gave her an innocent look. 'Why, the same thing you are, Margaret. It's all for the sake of sweet charity.' Now that the first dreadful moment was over, she was beginning to enjoy herself. 'Is William here?'

'Answer me!' Margaret demanded. 'What's going on?'

'Nothing's going on,' Paula murmured demurely. 'Matthew asked me to go with him tonight, and I accepted. I thought you'd be pleased.'

'Well, of course,' Margaret spluttered weakly. 'I am pleased. It's what I've been trying to get you to do for months, but. . .' Her voice trailed off.

Paula smiled sweetly, enjoying her sister's discomfiture. She knew quite well that Margaret's only objection to her appearance here tonight on the arm of Matthew Stratton was that she hadn't engineered the whole thing herself.

Margaret leaned back in her chair, now, and gave Paula a long searching look. 'Well,' she said at last, 'you are a deep one.' There was something like admiration in her voice. 'You've managed to walk off with the most eligible man in Washington all by yourself. How long has this been going on?'

Paula hesitated. She had promised herself when she decided to accept Matthew's strange proposition that she would avoid deliberate falsehoods. She would only tell the truth and let Margaret and others assume what they liked from what she didn't say.

'You could say that we first became really acquainted that night last December when I gave him a lift back to town from your dinner party. He lives in the same building I do, you know, and one thing just led to another.'

This seemed to satisfy Margaret, and by now the music had stopped and the rest of their party began drifting back to the table from the dance floor. The tables all seated eight people, and Paula soon saw that it was exactly the same party that was at the reception last year when she first met Matthew.

This time, however, David Wyatt was escorting Michele Lathrop, both of whom gave Paula a curious look as they sat down at the table, greeting her casually. Soon the Pittingers joined them, and William came along soon afterwards bearing a tray of drinks in his hands. Matthew was right behind him carrying two glasses.

'Paula,' William said, as soon as he spotted her, 'how nice to see you.' He set the tray down on the table and kissed her on the cheek.

'Hallo, William,' she said.

Then Matthew sat down beside her. He leaned towards her and one long arm moved casually over the back of her chair, not quite touching her.

'I know you like champagne, Paula,' he said clearly. 'I hope it's what you wanted. There's quite a crush at the bar.'

No one said a word. Paula could palpably feel the interested glances of the rest of the party at Matthew's possessive tone. 'Thank you,' she murmured, and took a deep swallow.

Then, blessedly, the music started up again. Matthew asked her to dance, and she jumped up gratefully, moving into his arms quickly, glad to get away from those inquisitive eyes at the table.

He held her decorously, at a distance, as they danced on the fringes of the crowded floor. 'Don't look so worried,' he said, looking down at her with a smile. 'The worst is over. We'll give them a chance to talk it over, and when we get back they'll be used to the idea. You'll see.'

She knew this was probably true, but she couldn't shake the little nagging worry at the back of her mind. 'I suppose you're right,' she said dubiously.

He gave her an appraising look. 'It's the deception that bothers you, isn't it?'

She nodded. 'I suppose so. Margaret may be a bully, but she really does care about me. I don't like to deliberately deceive her. Or William.'

'Just don't lie to them,' he said, moving further into the centre of the floor. 'Let them draw their own conclusions.'

It was more crowded here, and Paula felt herself being pushed from behind towards Matthew, so that her body was soon moulded firmly up against his long length. The sudden unexpected intimacy gave her a strange, breathless sensation.

She glanced up at him through her heavily fringed eyelashes, but he seemed to be staring off into space, preoccupied, lost in a world of his own. Someone jostled her again from behind, and she stumbled awkwardly. His arm tightened around her, his palm flat against her back as he pulled her closer in a protective gesture. She could feel the tips of his fingers resting on her bare back, just above the low cut bodice, and a brilliant wave of warmth swept over her.

Suddenly, irrelevantly, she thought about the night she had driven him home from Margaret's dinner party. He had been drunk, she knew, and had forgotten what he'd done until she reminded him the next day. She believed she had put it out of her own mind. Now, however, as he held her, she remembered it all quite clearly, the way his mouth had felt on hers, his hand on her breast, and the intensity of her feeling astonished her.

She pulled away slightly and gave him a more direct look. His face was grim and set, but he appeared to be entirely unmoved by the close contact. 'Can we go back to the table now?' she pleaded. 'This crowd is getting to me.'

He nodded and they started to make their way around the dancing couples back to their table. He wasn't touching her now, but she was quite conscious that he was right behind her and almost painfully aware of the strong body that pressed up against hers momentarily from time to time.

After that she danced once with a beaming William, delighted as he put it, to see her 'come out of her shell at last', and once with David Wyatt, subdued and respectful. By his manner, she could tell that he was impressed by her conquest of the elusive Matthew Stratton, even though his name wasn't mentioned.

Sitting at the table between dances, Paula was uncomfortably conscious of the hostile glances shot her way by a disgruntled Michele, gorgeous in a gold lamé dress that just matched her flowing blonde hair and clung to her sensational figure as though it had been poured on.

Throughout the rest of the evening, Matthew was attentive and courteous. He chatted easily with the others, danced with each woman in turn, and seemed more relaxed than Paula had ever seen him before. She realised, too, that she herself felt far more at ease in a social situation than she had since Richard's death. The others seemed to accept her fictitious 'relationship' with Matthew easily and naturally, just as he had predicted.

Gazing at him from time to time, she couldn't help puzzling over the odd sensations she had experienced in his arms on the dance floor. Finally, she came to the conclusion that they were most likely caused by her nervousness at their first public appearance together, the champagne she had drunk, the overcrowded floor.

Certainly, Matthew hadn't seemed to be bothered by any undercurrent of feeling. His behaviour throughout the evening was impeccable, and as they drove home later, he seemed as remote and contained as ever, treating her with an aloof courtesy that finally put her apprehensions to rest.

On their way up in the elevator to the apartment, she asked him if he had noticed Margaret's speechless reaction to their appearance at the ball together. He was vastly amused.

'Yes,' he said with a smile. 'Poor Margaret.'

Paula snorted as they walked down the hall to her door. 'Poor Margaret, nothing! She deserved it.' Putting her key in the lock, she couldn't suppress a wicked chuckle. 'She was only put out because she hadn't masterminded the whole thing herself.'

She turned to him now, suddenly shy. It was an awkward moment. Surely, she decided finally, the terms of their agreement didn't include late night tête-à-têtes alone in her apartment.

'Well, good night, then, Paula,' he said easily after she had stepped inside and turned on the light. 'It's been an enjoyable evening.'

'Yes, it has,' she murmured. 'Thank you very much.'

Without another word he was gone. Perversely, now that he had made the decision to leave, she felt a little twinge of disappointment. She closed the door quietly, took off her coat and hung it up in the hall closet, pondering this unexpected reaction to his abrupt withdrawal. That was what she wanted, wasn't it? She decided that it must be merely that her female vanity was wounded. She simply was not accustomed to such indifference.

She went into the bedroom and sat down on the edge of the bed, easing her shoes off her tired feet. She glanced over at Richard's photograph on the bedside table, the laughing dark eyes, the infectious grin, the smooth hair, and wondered how she could ever have thought that first night that there was any resemblance between Matthew Stratton and her dead husband.

Except that they were both tall, well-built and dark, they were as different as two men could be. For one thing, Richard had been several years younger, not yet thirty, with a boyish charm and outgoing ebullient personality. Matthew was at least thirty-six, she guessed, and much more reserved. He seldom even smiled, and then never with his eyes.

A familiar ache began to grow in the region of her heart, a powerful longing to have Richard's arms around her again, to feel him lying beside her in the cold empty bed. Their life together had been perfect, she thought now as the tears welled up. Richard had been a sweet gentle lover, and she had responded to him—the only man in her life— like a trusting child.

She shivered a little, then, as the image of Matthew Stratton intruded, stern and impressive. Unbidden, surprising her with its intensity, the

thought leapt into her mind that this man would
be a far more demanding and imperious lover than
her young husband.

Well, she thought, as she undressed and got into
bed, she'd never find out if that was true. He had
made it quite clear that he meant what he said in
his original proposition. Their relationship was to
be a mutual defence against other entanglements, a
social convenience, and that was all.

In the weeks that followed, Paula saw Matthew at
least once a week when he was in town. Like all
elected officials, he had to do a great deal of
travelling and was often gone for several days at a
time.

Even when he was gone, however, their
arrangement protected her. It was common
knowledge in Washington social circles by now
that they were always paired off. There had been
one or two thinly veiled items about them in the
gossip column of the large daily newspaper, and
their exclusive relationship seemed to be an
accepted fact.

Paula found this protection a great relief. She no
longer had to make excuses to Margaret as to why
she didn't want to go out with the latest eligible
man her sister unearthed. When Matthew was
gone, she could now go to parties unescorted
without bringing down Margaret's wrath. Senators
were quite highly placed in the hierarchy of power
in Washington, both politically and socially, and
once it became known that she and Matthew had
some kind of attachment, Paula became off limits
for the predators that prowled around the fringes
of the capital's social scene.

They did everything together, attending any

event that arose where she needed an escort or he needed a female companion. Their appearances remained public, however. They never went anywhere alone or unobserved. He had never set foot in her apartment again, even though they only lived three floors away from each other.

Their 'arrangement' had been in effect for about three months when it began to dawn on Paula that although they exchanged a great deal of information about each other, she didn't really know him any better now that she had at the beginning.

She knew she liked him, liked being with him, but he seemed to have erected invisible barriers around the core of himself, barriers Paula was too sensitive to try to breach. She had barriers of her own, she had to admit at last, and was satisfied with things as they were, for the most part.

Still, when at odd times he simply withdrew and the grey eyes took on an even more distant look, or in the middle of a conversation he would suddenly be gone, she couldn't help feeling a little hurt. She could only surmise that he still missed his wife, and would think of that evening in his apartment when he had mistaken her for Beth. It was hard to believe that this remote stranger was the same man who had held her then with such a depth of passion and desire.

It was April now, spring at last. The dingy remnants of winter's ice and snow had melted, the cherry blossoms were in bloom, and on sunny days women had begun tentatively to appear on the streets of the nation's capital in colourful summery dresses.

Margaret came into town one Monday for her weekly shopping expedition, and Paula had agreed to have lunch with her. She had offered to cook a meal at the apartment, but Margaret firmly vetoed that plan, as Paula knew she would. Margaret's trips into the city were primarily information-gathering forays. In order to keep current with the latest gossip, it was essential to see and be seen, and that meant a compulsory appearance at one of the more fashionable restaurants in town.

They met there at noon, and now that Paula was no longer the target of Margaret's battle plans, she found herself watching her sister in action with grudging admiration. The bright hazel eyes darted into every corner of the large crowded dining room, but so cleverly and unobtrusively that only the most practised eye could detect what she was doing.

All the while she carried on a chatty running commentary about which couple was on the verge of divorce, which congressman was in trouble with his constituency, which cabinet member was about to resign.

Paula could only sit and marvel at the way Margaret seemed to pick up all this information out of the air. Did they use sign language? she wondered. Smoke signals? Inaudible tomtoms?

It wasn't until dessert that Paula felt her sister's attention finally turn on her. The restaurant was half-empty by now, and the subtle communications seemed to have ceased.

'Now,' Margaret said briskly, sampling a bite of the restaurant's famous cheesecake, 'tell me what you've been up to.'

'Oh, the usual,' Paula replied idly. 'Working hard. I got a new commission from a store in Baltimore.' She had been thrilled when the offer came, her first from out of town.

'Oh, work,' Margaret said, dismissing it with a little wave of her fork. 'I mean you and Matthew.'

Paula tensed immediately and forced a smile. 'You just saw us last week at the Pittingers' anniversary party. Nothing has changed since then.'

'What do you mean by that?' Margaret probed. 'Please define for me the "nothing" that hasn't changed.'

'Oh, Margaret, we've been all over this before. Matthew and I are just friends. We enjoy each other's company.'

Paula knew she was on shaky ground. Discussing her personal life with Margaret was something like picking one's way through a minefield. One wrong word, and she'd set off an explosion of questions and unwanted advice.

'Oh, really?' Margaret drawled. 'Well, then, I'd say you'd either better get beyond the point of friendship with him or find someone else.' She eyed Paula with suspicion, her fork poised in the air. 'I have the distinct feeling you're hiding something from me. There's more going on between you and Senator Matthew Stratton than mere friendship.'

Paula flushed guiltily, thinking about the odd mutual protective society she and Matthew were involved in. 'Well,' she muttered at last, 'that's our business, isn't it?'

Margaret set down her fork. 'I knew it,' she crowed. 'I just knew it. It's serious, isn't it? Oh, darling, I'm so happy for you.'

Paula was aghast. Margaret had completely misunderstood her. Gazing now at the triumphant look on her sister's face, she was torn between firmly disabusing her of the notion that there was a serious romance going on between her and Matthew and letting her think what she pleased.

Either way, she thought, meant trouble, and since she could never hope to fool Margaret for long, she decided that honesty would be by far the most prudent policy.

'You're jumping to conclusions, as usual, Margaret,' she said in a positive tone. 'I'm going to say it just once more. Matthew and I are friends. That's all.'

'I don't believe you,' came the firm reply. 'I know you. You were the same with Richard, wouldn't tell me a thing until you were ready to announce your engagement.' Paula opened her mouth to protest again, but Margaret raised a hand and droned inexorably on. 'That's all right. You don't have to say a word. You always were a deep one.'

Paula sighed. It was like trying to stop a Sherman tank with a popgun. 'I'm telling you the truth,' she said weakly.

Margaret reached across the table then and covered Paula's hand with hers. 'It's all right, darling,' she said with real affection. 'I only want you to be happy. Don't worry. I won't interfere and spoil it for you.' The hazel eyes grew misty with sentiment. 'William and I would both love it, though, if you were to get married at our place. June, perhaps, when the garden is so lovely.'

'Margaret, you're way ahead of yourself. Please, believe me. . .'

'Of course, darling, not another word.' She glanced at her watch. 'Oh, dear, I must run. We're having guests for dinner and I have a million things to do.'

Paula had a light supper alone in her apartment that night. She sat on a stool at the kitchen counter over a bowl of soup, leafing through the evening paper. She hardly ever read the news articles in any depth, but she did like to skim over the fashion illustrations to see what the competition was doing.

The most important of these were on the society page, where women were sure to browse. As she carefully examined her chief rival's drawings, her eye was suddenly caught by her name in the lead item of the most persistent and outrageous of the gossip columnists.

'All Washington is on pins and needles to see when wedding bells will chime for the charming senator from Maryland, Matthew Stratton, and his constant companion, the lovely young widow, Paula Waring. Mrs Waring is the sister-in-law of William Chandler, prominent member of the President's personal staff.'

Paula blanched as she read the article over again more carefully. Really, this was too much! Wasn't it invasion of privacy? She felt naked, exposed, humiliated. But what could she do? Call the paper and demand a retraction?

She threw down the paper and began pacing the room. 'Constant companion!' she fumed. She knew quite well what that meant. The phrase was a shopworn euphemism for mistress. She stopped short as a dreadful suspicion came to her. Would Margaret have done such a terrible thing? Given that damned columnist 'inside information', information she had dreamed up herself?

No, she decided, resuming her pacing. Margaret would never go that far. Besides, what difference did it make? she thought, literally wringing her hands in frustration. The damage was done now anyway.

Oh, I'd like to throttle that columnist, she groaned to herself. What a despicable way to make a living! Victimising people like that, smearing their names with lies, ruining reputations, spoiling innocent relationships.

That was the worst of it, she realised. The pleasant arrangement with Matthew was tarnished, irrevocably spoiled. She could never be seen with him again, she knew, without the terrible thought that everyone in Washington believed they were having an affair. Her reputation was ruined, and certainly it wouldn't do Matthew's career any good to be publicly branded that way.

The doorbell rang. Still angry, she flounced to the door and flung it open. Matthew was standing there, solemn-faced, a newspaper in his hand.

'I see you've read it,' she said bitterly, her green eyes flashing. 'Come in.'

She turned and stalked into the living room. She heard the door close quietly, then the sound of his footsteps behind her. When she whirled around to face him, the expression on his face was unreadable, the grey eyes stony.

'I know what you're thinking,' she began, calming herself with an effort, 'and I'm sure it wasn't Margaret.'

He drew in a deep breath and then exhaled slowly. 'Do you have anything to drink?' he asked.

'I don't see how you can stand there so calmly,' she accused, pointing at the newspaper he was carrying, 'when both our reputations are ruined.'

'Calm down, Paula,' he said, advancing slowly towards her, 'and let's talk about it. May I sit down?'

He seemed to be taking it so coolly, she thought, as she gestured impatiently toward the long rust-coloured sofa. Perhaps it wasn't as bad as she thought. He spread out the newspaper on the coffee table in front of him and gazed down at it, ignoring her.

She went into the kitchen and poured them both a stiff scotch and soda. Maybe she had overreacted, she thought, as she brought the drinks back into the living room. She handed him his glass and sat down beside him, waiting to hear what he had to say.

He took a long swallow of scotch, then turned to her. 'I was expecting something like this. Several people have given me pretty broad hints lately about the status of our. . .' He hesitated, then smiled fleetingly, 'Our affair.'

'But there is no affair,' she protested hotly. 'You're a senator. Can't you call that columnist and make him retract the statement? "Constant companion!" You know what that means, don't you?'

'Yes,' he replied evenly. 'I know what that means.'

She jumped to her feet and began to pace the room. 'Well, the whole thing has backfired. When I agreed to your proposition, I had no idea that people would get the impression we were . . . were . . . lovers.' She glared at him accusingly. 'I've taken great pains since Richard's death to preserve a good reputation. That's not easy to do in this town, especially when you have Margaret throwing men at you, and now. . .'

'Sit down, Paula,' his voice rang out with authority. She stopped her pacing and stared at him, wide-eyed, shocked at his tone. 'Please,' he said in a gentler voice. She obeyed and sank slowly down beside him on the sofa, gazing sullenly at her drink.

'I think I have a solution,' he said at last. 'We'll get married.'

CHAPTER FIVE

SLOWLY Paula raised her eyes from the glass in her hand and stared at him. 'Married!' she exclaimed. 'You must be joking! How can we get married?'

'Simple,' he said. 'We get a licence and just do it.'

'That isn't what I meant!' she snapped.

'I know what you meant.' He drained his glass and set it down on the coffee table.

Paula's head was reeling. She was having trouble breathing. Married! What was he thinking of? A nasty little item in the gossip column was one thing, a lifetime commitment to a man she didn't love, who didn't love her, quite another.

She finally collected herself enough to speak calmly. 'Isn't that a little extreme?' she asked with a wry smile. 'Wouldn't it be simpler to just call off the whole arrangement?'

He turned then to face her, solemn-eyed and grave. 'Is that what you want, Paula? Do you want to go back to dealing with your sister's interference, fending off passes?'

'Well, no,' she said weakly, 'but I don't want. . .' She reddened, unable to go on.

'Before you make up your mind,' he broke in, 'perhaps I'd better explain more clearly what I have in mind.'

'Please do,' she murmured. She had the uneasy feeling that she was being drawn into a situation that was way over her head.

She looked at Matthew. He seemed to be deep in thought. She knew by now the way his mind worked. He was never impulsive, never acted thoughtlessly. He wouldn't speak now unless he had it all worked out in his mind just what he wanted to say.

As she waited, she began to wonder what it would be like to be married to this tall, remote man. What would he expect of her? Did she want to give up her freedom on any terms?

'What I have in mind,' he said at last, 'is really just an extension of our original arrangement. From my point of view, it worked beautifully until this came along.' He nodded towards the offending newspaper, still lying on the coffee table. 'Do you agree?'

'Yes, I do.' It was the truth. She really had enjoyed being with him and appreciated the security, the protection. 'But. . .'

He held up a hand. 'Let me finish. I want you to understand how I feel before you make up your mind. I don't see any remote possibility of falling in love again. I've already told you that. But I do need a wife in my position.' He frowned. 'That sounds so cold-blooded, and I don't mean it that way. I've come to be very fond of you, Paula,' he went on, the grey eyes softer now. 'I like being with you. We enjoy doing the same things, have the same way of looking at life. Our backgrounds are similar. If my understanding is correct, you're no more interested in a grand passion than I am.' He paused, his eyes asking a question.

'No,' she said promptly. 'I'm not.' There was one thing he hadn't mentioned, one thing she had to understand before she could even begin to make a decision on his strange proposal. She took a deep breath and looked directly into his eyes. 'What would you expect from me?'

His dark eyebrows shot up. For once she had caught him off guard, and she felt a strange surge of satisfaction flow through her. He was too calm and collected. It pleased her to see him even slightly ruffled.

'Nothing physical, of course,' he replied stiffly. 'I assumed that was understood.'

She leaned back on the couch, enjoying his discomfiture. 'Won't you find that difficult at such close quarters?' she asked in a slightly mocking tone. 'Or do you plan on having affairs?'

A dark flush spread over his features. She could tell she had made him angry, and it exhilarated her to see that she could stir some emotion in him. Maybe he'd call the whole thing off. She didn't care.

She could see that he was controlling himself with an effort. His fists were clenched on his knees, and a little pulse beat erratically at his temple just where the neatly combed black hair began.

Then he relaxed visibly and smiled. 'No,' he replied. 'I don't plan on having affairs. Do you?'

'No,' she muttered, taken aback. 'Of course not. I'm sorry. I had no right to say that.'

'You had every right,' he shot back firmly. 'If we decide to go ahead with this, I want to be sure your interests are considered every bit as much as mine, and even though it would technically be only a marriage of convenience, I want you to know I'd never do anything to embarrass you.'

He paused for a moment, then went on. 'After Beth died, I admit I went off the deep end for a while. I guess I was looking for her in other women. Something like that, anyway. Apparently, I got it out of my system because after a year or so, I managed to get hold of myself, decided to put my energies into public service, my political career. The meaningless affairs were far more trouble than they were worth.'

Paula didn't know what to say. She just sat there staring down at her hands in her lap. The offer was tempting. She wasn't looking for love, but it would be nice to have security. Maybe, eventually, if it worked out, they could even adopt children.

Richard had been dead over a year, and with each passing month her conviction that she would never fall in love again only strengthened. She thought back to the bleak grey days before Matthew came into her life, and she knew she didn't want to go back to that dreary emptiness.

She considered her alternatives. She knew she had only two choices. She could enter into a marriage of convenience with Matthew or she could give up his friendship. In either case, love would be missing, but since her capacity to love seemed to have died with Richard anyway, at least as Matthew's wife she'd have something.

She turned to face him. 'All right, Matthew,' she said calmly, her mind made up. 'I'll marry you.'

Margaret, of course, was ecstatic, and immediately began making elaborate plans for a June garden wedding at the Chandler home in Virginia.

'Sorry, Margaret,' Paula said firmly over dinner a week later. 'No big wedding.'

'And we're not waiting until June,' Matthew put in.

Paula shot him a quick look across the long dining table. He sounded just like an impatient bridegroom, she thought. He must be a better actor than she had given him credit for.

William spoke up from the head of the table, forestalling Margaret's objections. 'Well, I hope you'll at least invite us to the ceremony. Where will you live?'

'I'll just move upstairs to Matthew's apartment,' Paula rushed on before her sister had the chance to take charge of the conversation. 'It's much larger than mine. There's an extra bedroom I can use for a studio.'

She neglected to mention that she would also be sleeping in that extra bedroom. It was no one's business how she and Matthew chose to conduct their marriage. They had worked it all out between them, and with each passing day, Paula felt more and more sure she was doing the right thing.

Matthew seemed to be bending over backwards to please her. He had insisted she take the larger of the two bedrooms, with its own private bath, and had promised her a free hand in redecorating, telling her to make whatever changes she liked. She planned to use most of her own furniture. Matthew had spartan tastes, only the bare essentials, since he did all his entertaining in restaurants.

She listened now as he went on to explain their plans to a subdued Margaret. 'One of the Supreme Court justices is an old friend of the family. He'll marry us in the Senate chapel, and of course we want you both there.'

Margaret was cowed by the authoritative tone, Paula could see, but wasn't going to give up without a struggle. 'It just doesn't seem right,' she grumbled. 'A United States Senator doesn't get married every day. Everyone in Washington will want to attend.'

'No one in Washington is going to attend,'

Matthew said firmly, 'because no one is going to know about it except you and my brother. After it's over, Margaret, perhaps you'd like to give a reception for us. In a week or two.'

Margaret's glum expression brightened at the bone thrown to her. She was an old hand at society infighting and knew when to concede graciously in exchange for a quid pro quo like that plum. She'd be the envy of all her friends. A reception for a newlywed senator was not quite the same as a wedding, but it was certainly the next best thing.

Paula watched her sister with amusement. She could almost see her ticking over in her mind who to invite, who to exclude, what to serve. Happy at last, she made no objection when Matthew glanced at his watch early and said they'd have to be going.

'She seemed almost glad to get rid of us,' Paula laughed on the way home. 'That was nice of you, Matthew, to let her have a reception. These things mean a lot to her.'

A week later, the wedding went off as planned. There were no reporters present and no guests except William and Margaret, who cried noisily throughout the whole ceremony, and Matthew's brother and his wife.

Paula felt oddly detached, as though she was standing aside watching herself standing there beside Matthew in front of Justice Monahan repeating her marriage vows. When it was over and Matthew leaned down and kissed her briefly, coolly on the lips, she was startled momentarily by the intimacy.

Of course, she knew the kiss was for the benefit

of the others. Still, when their glance met, after it was over, she thought she could see a new warmth in the silvery eyes. They smiled at each other, and Paula felt a sudden strong surge of affection for this tall, honourable man.

Even though it wouldn't be a real marriage, she thought, he had placed enormous power over him in her hands. By giving her his name, his public protection, he was trusting her with his career, his future, and much of his well-being.

I'll be a good wife to him, she thought fiercely to herself, just as I know he'll be a good husband to me. Mutual trust and simple friendship were just as good a basis for marriage as love and passion, she reasoned. Perhaps a better one. They'd both loved and lost once, been shattered by it, and never wanted to risk it again. It would be all right.

They had decided against a honeymoon. Congress was in session, and Matthew, as a new senator, felt he owed it to his constituency to be present every day. Besides, the unspoken thought between them was of the awkwardness of staying in a resort or hotel when they didn't plan to share a bedroom.

After the early evening ceremony, William insisted on taking the whole party out to dinner. Paula was glad. She wanted to delay as long as possible their first awkward night together.

She was charmed by Matthew's brother, Andrew, four years older and more extrovert. He and Marsha, his wife, seemed to be delighted at the marriage, and welcomed Paula warmly into the Stratton family.

'Well, Mrs Stratton,' Margaret whispered to her as they parted after dinner, 'be happy.' There were tears in her eyes as she hugged Paula.

'Sentimental idiot,' Paula muttered, forcing a smile. She felt like a fraud.

William dropped them at the Georgetown apartment, and when they got into the elevator, Paula automatically reached out to punch the third floor button.

'You don't live there any more, remember?' Matthew said easily, reaching past her to punch the sixth floor.

He looked down at her with an amused smile. She reddened and pulled her hand away quickly. 'Of course,' she murmured. 'How stupid of me.'

They rode up to the sixth floor in silence, then walked down the hall together to Matthew's apartment. *My* apartment, too, now, she thought to herself. She felt strangely disoriented, even a little lightheaded.

When they went inside and she saw her own things in the living room, where they had been moved from downstairs the previous week, her head began to clear. It would be all right, she thought, once the first awkwardness was over.

'Would you like a drink?' Matthew asked. He crossed over to the windows to draw the curtains shut. 'A cup of coffee?'

'No, thanks.' Her voice sounded a little wobbly. 'I'm rather tired. I think I'll turn in, if you don't mind.' The tremor in her voice only got worse. I've got to get out of here, she thought wildly to herself. I've got to be alone.

Matthew came to stand before her. She couldn't read his feelings from the impassive face and distant grey eyes, but when he spoke, his voice was gently mocking. 'Wedding night jitters, Paula?'

Her eyes flew open and she took a step back

from him. Immediately, his grey eyes narrowed
and a frown appeared on the fine features.

'Hey,' he said. 'I'm only joking.' Then he smiled.
'You *are* jumpy. Sure you don't want that drink?
Come on, I'll light the fire.'

Reluctantly, she agreed, and as they settled on
the sofa in front of the flickering fire sipping
drinks, she gradually began to relax. Matthew had
told her to choose some music, and on an impulse
she put on the Haydn cello concerto.

Matthew had taken off his jacket and loosened
his tie. He sat now with his long legs stretched out
before him, his head leaning back, his eyes closed.
By the light of the flickering fire, Paula watched
him. He seemed to be almost asleep, lulled by the
gentle strains of the Haydn.

This man is my husband, she thought, still not
quite believing she had actually gone through with
the marriage. The firelight cast dancing shadows
on the flat planes of his cheeks and strong jaw.
The crisp dark hair was a little untidy and he had
rolled the sleeves of his white shirt up, revealing
strong forearms, lightly covered with fine dark hair.

She knew he would never hurt her, never
wilfully cause her pain. As the fire and the scotch
she was drinking warmed her, she slowly began to
thaw and allowed her mind to wander. She looked
at his hands, large and strong with long tapering
fingers, and found herself wondering how they
would feel touching her.

He opened his eyes then and turned his head
lazily towards her. 'Feeling better?'

She jumped a little, then smiled at him. 'Much
better. It just doesn't seem quite real to me yet.'

'It'll be all right, Paula. You'll see.'

*   *   *

After they had survived, with rueful amusement, Margaret's spectacular 'reception', Paula settled easily into her new life, probably, she thought, because it wasn't much different from her old one. Surrounded by her own belongings, hard at work on her drawings, even living in the same building, the pattern of her days was much the same as it had always been.

Matthew, of course, was gone a great deal, and even when he was at home their lives were separate. Although they ate their meals together and attended social affairs as a couple, they lived almost like strangers who happened to share the same apartment.

Paula considered Matthew's bedroom sacrosanct, as he did hers, and for the first two weeks of their marriage she didn't even glance inside as she passed by it. One day, however, her curiosity got the better of her, and she decided it couldn't do any harm just to take a quick look. She knew Matthew wouldn't care, and nursed the faint hope that the room might reveal some clue as to her remote husband's inner life.

She was quickly disabused of that notion. Except for a pair of cufflinks on the dresser and a tie hanging over a chair, the room was as impersonal as if it had been in a hotel. The double bed was neatly made, and only the large oak desk in the far corner showed any signs of personal use.

Then she saw the photograph on the bedside table and knew, of course, that it was Beth. Drawn by an overpowering curiosity, she moved over to the side of the bed and looked down at the smiling face of a young, fair-haired woman. She was breathtakingly beautiful, Paula thought, with delicate features and a fragile air of mystery in the slight smile, the turn of the head. The overall impression was one of the eternal feminine, elusive and serene.

Paula felt a sudden sharp stab of jealousy. Recovering herself immediately, she quickly walked back out into the hall and almost ran to the sanctuary of her own bedroom. What had got into her? She picked up Richard's photograph and gazed into the warm dark eyes.

'It's you I love,' she whispered, hugging the picture to her. 'I haven't been unfaithful. I'm not really married, and I certainly feel nothing for the dark, cold-eyed stranger who happens to be my husband.'

At the wedding dinner, Matthew had promised his brother that he and Paula would spend the Easter weekend in May with them at the farm in Maryland. It would also be a good opportunity for him to spend some time in his constituency.

'Mending fences,' he said to Paula as they drove through the rolling hills of northern Virginia into southern Maryland on the Thursday afternoon before Easter.

The apple blossoms were in full bloom now, perfuming the warm spring air with their heady fragrance, acres and acres of them as far as the eye could see on either side of the winding road.

They had been married a little over a month, and glancing at him now as he drove, Paula realised that she didn't know her husband any better now than she had before their wedding. Well, that was the bargain, the arrangement, she told herself, and she was generally content with it.

The Stratton family home was set in a wide

valley near the southern border of Pennsylvania. It was a sprawling white farmhouse with well-kept stables surrounded by acres of orchard and pasture.

Paula warmed immediately to Marsha, her new sister-in-law, and while the two men rode out to inspect the horses, they sat outside on the wide flagstone terrace drinking iced tea.

'I'm so glad you could come,' Marsha said after they had settled themselves at the round glass-topped table. 'I've been dying to get to know you better.'

Paula was amused at her frankness. She was a short, plump, friendly woman with untidy faded blonde hair and an infectious smile. All her movements were brisk and assured, and Paula found herself wondering how she and Margaret would get along. They were much alike.

'It's a lovely old place,' she commented. 'And so well cared for. Have you lived here all your married life?'

'Oh, yes. We even spent our honeymoon here. Mustn't leave the horses, you know. At least, that's Andrew's excuse. He hates to travel. We have a perfectly good stable manager and trainer, but,' she shrugged, 'my husband is convinced the place would fall apart without his personal supervision.'

'Where is your little girl?' Paula asked. 'My sister has two children, both boys, and when they were younger, it seemed they were always underfoot—and highly audible.'

Marsha laughed. 'Oh, Laurie is no shrinking violet. How could she be with such noisy parents? She's at a birthday party this afternoon. One of the neighbours will bring her home before dinner.

She was quite torn between going to the party and being here when Uncle Matthew arrived. She dotes on him.'

Uncle Matthew, Paula thought. It sounded so strange. 'How old is Laurie?'

'She's six.' Marsha grinned at the look of surprise Paula couldn't quite hide. 'I know what you're thinking. How come two old fogies like Andrew and I produced a child on the fringes of middle-age.'

Paula murmured a feeble protest, but had to admit to herself that Marsha was right. Andrew had to be forty, and Marsha was not much younger.

'We waited a long time for Laurie,' Marsha explained, suddenly sober. She gave Paula a cautious look. 'It's none of my business, but I hope you and Matthew have better luck. He'd make a wonderful father.'

'Yes, he would,' Paula agreed automatically. Then it came to her with a little shock that Marsha was right. Matthew would be a fine father.

'Beth never wanted children, you know,' Marsha went on. 'Perhaps Matthew didn't either. I wouldn't know.' She smiled. 'He keeps his feelings pretty much to himself, as you've no doubt discovered. At any rate,' she went on, 'he was just getting started in his political career, so it may have been a mutual agreement.' She paused, as if not sure of her ground. 'She was very beautiful, you know,' she said slowly at last. 'Beth. Rather fragile, if you understand what I mean.'

'I've seen her picture,' Paula said. The conversation was making her vaguely uneasy, as if they were talking behind Matthew's back. 'I agree. She was quite lovely. I know Matthew loved her very much.'

'Too much, I sometimes thought,' Marsha said, her voice tinged with bitterness. 'Beth liked to create an air of mystery about her. She was an elusive creature.' She stared directly at Paula now. 'And totally selfish.'

Paula shifted uncomfortably in her chair. 'Marsha . . .' she began, wanting to put an end to the conversation, but afraid of hurting the other woman's feelings.

'Oh, I know,' Marsha broke in. 'Shouldn't speak ill of the dead. I just want you to know that I'm delighted Matthew married again, and to someone so different from Beth. You're obviously a giving person, warm and loving, just what he needed to break Beth's hold on him once and for all. If he fell in love with you, that tells me her spell must be finally exorcised.' She smiled warmly.

Andrew and Matthew appeared just then, back from their ride, and a few minutes later Laurie returned home from her party. Caught up in the ensuing commotion, Paula was relieved that her conversation with Marsha was cut off, but during the rest of their stay she found herself returning to it again and again.

Of course, Marsha had no way of knowing that Matthew was not in love with her, and was actually still quite firmly held by the spell of his dead wife. Was it a spell? she wondered. Could it be broken?

Seeing Matthew with his family showed Paula an entirely new side of him. The iron reserve she had become so accustomed to seemed to crack and gradually disappear. Andrew and Marsha, both so outgoing, brought out a lighthearted aspect of Matthew's nature that Paula had not known existed.

Over coffee that first evening after dinner, Andrew suggested that she might like to go down to the stable to see the horses.

She frowned. 'I don't know. I've never been around horses.' She looked at Matthew. 'I'm a city girl, remember?' The truth was, she was afraid of the great beasts, but didn't like to say so.

Matthew grinned. 'They won't bite. They're really quite gentle creatures.' He was leaning back in the sturdy captain's chair, one ankle crossed over his other knee, relaxed and happy. He had on a well-worn pair of blue jeans and a plaid flannel shirt, and Paula saw that the customary lines of tension on his face were smoothed away.

'Besides,' Andrew said, 'they're all in their stalls and can't get out.' He was gazing at her with amusement in his dark eyes.

Paula gave him a dubious look. He was sitting next to Matthew, dressed in almost identical clothes, and pretty much the same size. Other than that, the two men were very different. Andrew's dark hair was shot with grey, his face was fuller, and his motions more abrupt and impatient.

Laurie had been staring, wide-eyed, at Paula throughout this exchange. Now she piped up. 'You're not afraid of horses, are you?' she asked in an incredulous tone.

'Well, no,' Paula fibbed, reddening. 'I'd like to see them.'

They set off down to the stables. Dusk had fallen, and the quiet countryside was peaceful and serene, the fragrance of apple blossoms heavy on the evening air.

Inside the stable, Laurie danced ahead down past the row of stalls, eager to show Paula her very own horse. She had been riding since she was three years old.

'His name is Prince,' she said proudly, pulling Paula by the hand over to a stall where a mild-looking, rather small horse with liquid brown eyes stood quietly munching hay.

The stable was warm and smelled damply of horses and straw. As she gingerly approached the stall, Paula began to feel braver. Prince *seemed* gentle enough.

'Now that you're in the family, Paula,' Andrew boomed from behind her, 'you're going to have to learn to ride.'

Paula turned around and stared at him. She bit her lip and glanced at Matthew, standing beside his brother. He smiled at her. 'There's no hurry,' he said easily. 'Whenever you're ready.'

Andrew had a bag of apples in his hand, which he had fed to each horse in turn in the long row. He held one out to Paula now.

'Here. You can give this to Prince. It's a good way to get acquainted.'

Paula didn't know what to do. Surely, if Andrew and Marsha let Laurie ride the horse, he must be gentle. She looked at the beautiful dappled animal. He looked quiet and friendly.

'All right,' she said, and took the apple from Andrew's outstretched hand.

She walked slowly towards Prince, who was eyeing her with interest. She held the apple out flat on the palm of her hand. Was she supposed to put it into that huge mouth? No, she decided, let him get it himself. He couldn't quite reach it, so she took one step closer to him, leaning forward tentatively.

At that moment, Prince chose to rear up

playfully on his hind legs and let out a loud whinny. Paula gave a little shriek, dropped the apple, and turned and ran straight into Matthew's arms.

She buried her face in his chest, clinging to the rough material of the plaid shirt, more embarrassed now than frightened. She could hear the others hooting with laughter, but Matthew only stroked her back soothingly, his arms strong and comforting around her.

Finally, she looked up at him, ashamed of her panicky flight, and beginning to laugh at herself along with the others.

'Sorry, Matthew,' she said, grinning. 'That must have been a comical sight. Have I disgraced you in front of your family?'

He was gazing down at her, still holding her, an odd look on his face. He put a hand flat on her cheek, warm and strong, and Paula felt a sudden glow at how cherished this protective gesture made her feel.

'No, he said, smiling. 'Nothing you could do would disgrace me.'

It was as though they were all alone in the vast stable for that one brief moment, but then it passed as suddenly as it came. Paula heard Laurie calling her name, urging her to try again, and when she felt Matthew's hands slowly leave her, she turned around.

'All right, you've had your fun,' she said. 'Give me another apple, and I'll show you that a city girl may be stupid about horses, but she's not afraid to try again.'

'Good girl!' Andrew shouted delightedly, and handed her another apple.

This time she succeeded, and when she stood

back and watched Prince contentedly munching the apple she had given him, she felt a sense of accomplishment and pride that astonished her with its intensity.

They went back to the house, then, still laughing at Paula's fright and congratulating her on her bravery. She was beginning to feel that she was a real part of this strong, affectionate family.

'We'll make a horsewoman of you yet,' Andrew boomed as he lit the fire in the enormous living room. 'You don't know anything about horses, but you've got guts.'

Laurie was bundled off to bed then, and Paula watched delightedly when the little girl climbed up onto Matthew's lap, put her arms around his neck and kissed him goodnight. Who would ever have believed that the stern Senator Stratton could be like putty in his niece's hands, she thought to herself when she saw the obvious pleasure light up his face.

They sat in front of the fire drinking cider and talking until midnight, when Andrew finally stood up abruptly, stretched and yawned, and announced that he didn't know about the rest of them, but he had to get up early the next morning and was going to bed.

'There are no weekends on a farm,' Marsha explained as she led the way upstairs to the bedrooms. 'There's no need for you and Matthew to get up early, though. Sleep as long as you like.'

They said goodnight then, and Paula and Matthew went into the bedroom that had been given to them earlier. Marsha had mentioned to her that it was Matthew's old room, and there were still vestiges in it from his boyhood, a model airplane hanging from the ceiling, a shelf full of adventure books on one wall, fishing gear in a corner.

The sleeping arrangements at the farm had worried Paula at first, but she soon saw that the problem was easily resolved by the fact that each bedroom had a sleeping porch attached to it. Matthew turned to her now and announced calmly that he would sleep out on the screened-in porch.

'We will have to share the bathroom,' he said with a humorous glint in the grey eyes, 'but I'm very neat. I hang up my own towels and always screw the top back on the toothpaste.'

Still, Paula was troubled. 'Won't Marsha realise what's going on when she sees that both beds have been slept in?'

Matthew only shrugged. 'Who cares? She won't say anything, and so long as we're satisfied with the arrangement, it's no one else's business.'

He was right, of course, she thought later as she lay in bed listening to the strange sounds of the country through the open window. There was a pond nearby, and the chirping and croaking of the frogs was almost deafening to her city-bred ears.

She was glad it wasn't Margaret's house they were staying in. Nothing escaped her! If they were to spend one night in separate beds under the same roof as her sister, she'd soon ferret out the truth and confront Paula with it.

It gave her an odd feeling to realise that Matthew was sleeping not ten feet from her out on the connecting porch. They had taken turns in the bathroom and managed to stay out of each other's way, avoiding any more intimacy than they shared in the apartment. It was all working out quite well. Wasn't it? she asked herself as she tossed and turned in the strange bed.

She thought about the way Matthew had held her, touched her, out in the stable that evening when she had been so frightened of the horse. As though we were really married, she mused, and she couldn't help wondering what it would be like to be his wife in every sense of the word.

Now, that's silly, she admonished herself, turning over once again. The arrangement they had was perfectly satisfactory to both of them. Matthew certainly didn't seem to want more, and neither did she. No one would ever take Richard's place in her heart. The habit of loving him was too strong ever to be broken.

'Did you enjoy the weekend?' Matthew asked as they drove back to Washington on Monday morning.

'Oh, yes, very much,' Paula replied, turning to him with a smile. 'I liked them both. They made me feel quite welcome.'

'Good. They liked you, too.' He met her glance briefly and smiled. 'Why shouldn't they? You're a very likeable person.'

Paula didn't know what to reply to that. She was glad to hear that Matthew found her likeable, but the words, so well-meant, left her feeling a little cold and empty.

'What's wrong, Paula?' she heard him ask.

'Nothing. Nothing at all,' she said quickly. 'I guess I'm just digesting the weekend.'

He nodded, his eyes on the road ahead. 'The three of them can be a little overpowering at times. Not quite our style, but probably good for us both once in a while.'

CHAPTER SIX

AFTER the weekend with Matthew's family, Paula began to notice a subtle change in their relationship. It was nothing she could put her finger on, just a vague tension, a feeling of strain between them, as though they were watching each other, moving and speaking more cautiously.

She found herself stopping by the open door of his bedroom more and more often during the day when she was home alone. She never went inside, but her eyes always travelled first to the bedside table, to the silver-framed photograph of Beth. Every time she saw it there, her heart sank, and she finally realised that secretly she hoped some day to find it gone.

This bothered her. She had enjoyed their old easy relationship. What had happened? Had Matthew changed? Had she? She kept thinking about that conversation with Marsha, what she had said about Beth, her blithe assumption that Matthew was in love with her and had put Beth out of his mind. What would she think if she knew the truth?

Their arrangement began to seem more and more like a deception to her, and this made her uncomfortable. One morning when Margaret had dropped in unexpectedly, she'd seen the unmade bed in Paula's room, the room she had claimed she used only as a studio. For once, Margaret hadn't asked any questions, but ever since then Paula had been aware of some strange, suspicious looks darted her way.

Matthew seemed to be spending more and more time away from home, and when he was there, at meals or in the evenings when he didn't have a meeting, his manner towards her was courteous, but distant. Yet, every once in a while, when she was reading beside him or watching television or listening to music, she could sense him watching her and could almost feel the intensity behind that brooding gaze.

One night in early June, about a month after their visit to the farm, Margaret once again produced two tickets to the Chandler box at Kennedy Center. By coincidence, the soloist was another cellist, a famous Russian expatriate, considered by some critics to be the greatest cellist since Pablo Casals.

Paula and Matthew sat at the back of the box again, and glancing through the programme before the concert began, Paula noticed that they were playing the same Haydn concerto as on that night last winter when she and Matthew had gone together.

She darted a brief look at Matthew, sitting beside her, to see if he'd noticed. Their eyes met, and they smiled conspiratorially at each other.

Suddenly, the past several weeks of tension seemed to melt away, and they were back on their old comradely footing. Matthew leaned towards her and spoke into her ear in a low voice.

'I notice we don't finish up with Bartók this time.'

She glanced back at her programme, then lifted her head so that her mouth was at his ear. 'No. It's Brahms. Much better. Shall we stay for the second half this time?'

Their faces were almost touching. Glancing sideways at him, Paula could see the way the skin

around his downcast eyes crinkled as he smiled,
listening to her. The thin mobile mouth twitched in
amusement.

'Yes,' he agreed. 'We owe them that much, after
ducking out on the Bartók. Besides, I'm very fond
of Brahms.'

Before she could answer, the houselights
dimmed and the conductor strode out on to the
stage. He bowed, mounted the podium, raised his
baton, and the concert began.

During the Haydn, Paula was lost again in the
poignant beauty of the larghetto. The Russian
cellist took it at a much slower tempo, the lower
tones deeply resonant, heartbreaking in their long,
drawn-out plangency. The tears gathered and
spilled over unnoticed this time.

She closed her eyes, so wrapped up in the music
that when she realised that Matthew's arm had
come around her shoulders, it seemed perfectly
natural to her, as though his touch on her bare
shoulders was all that was needed to perfect the
mood the music evoked.

She leaned her head back against his sheltering
arm and felt his fingers tighten on her shoulder.
Their bodies were touching now and a warmth
stole through Paula at the intimate contact. It was
a perfect moment, she thought. Even the tears
were pleasant.

At the end of the larghetto, Matthew reached
into his breast pocket, took out a handkerchief
and gently wiped the tears away. He handed it to
her then, and she quietly blew her nose. She
looked at him, and in the darkened hall she could
still make out the smile on his face, the gleaming
of the silvery eyes.

When the lights came up at the intermission, the

intimate mood passed. They went out into the lobby for a drink, met a colleague of Matthew's there with his wife, and stood there chatting with them until the five-minute gong rang.

For the rest of the concert and on the way home, Matthew seemed to withdraw into himself again, and after that evening, that one brief moment when they had been so close, the familiar pattern of polite distance between them was resumed.

Paula found herself becoming more and more confused, about Matthew's feelings and her own. She began to feel jumpy around him. He seemed to be avoiding her, yet she would still catch one of those brooding looks fastened on her from time to time.

It happened mostly when they were alone, but occasionally when they were at a party or a dinner some force would draw her glance across the room to find him staring at her. He would smile briefly, casually, and look away, but she was always left feeling vaguely unsettled.

Finally, she began to wonder if he was having an affair. He had said he would never embarrass her publicly, and she knew he would keep his word, but he could be quietly involved with a woman and no one would know.

She tried not to let herself dwell on these speculations. After all, they didn't have a real marriage, and just the few glimpses she had had of the warmth and passion simmering beneath Matthew's cool, remote exterior told her that he had a normal man's desires.

As the weeks passed, they seemed to be drifting farther and farther apart, had less and less to say to each other. Her work was beginning to suffer under the constant tension, and finally, by the middle of summer, Paula made up her mind to confront him, to find out once and for all what was on his mind.

It was an especially warm evening in mid-July when she decided it was time to speak to him. He had been particularly silent over dinner and had excused himself shortly afterwards to go shower and change his clothes. He had a meeting that night, and as she cleared the table, Paula wondered if she should initiate a conversation before he left, or wait up for him and have it out with him when he came home. Better wait, she thought, no matter how late he was.

After he left for his meeting, she sat in the living room and began to rehearse in her mind what she would say to him. She wanted above all to be calm, to give him a chance to back out of the marriage gracefully if that's what he wanted, with no regrets on either side, no recriminations. If there was another woman, perhaps he'd really fallen in love again, and she wanted him to have that chance at happiness. She'd miss him, miss his company, but anything would be better than this strained silence.

She was still sitting there, idly turning the pages of a magazine, when she heard his key in the lock less than an hour after he'd left. When he came inside, she looked up at him, surprised to see him back so soon. She was nowhere near prepared with her speech.

'I decided not to go to the meeting,' he said. 'They can manage without me.'

She stared at him. He was leaning back against the door, a haggard look on his face. He seemed strangely unkempt to her, his tie slightly askew, his jacket hanging in the crook of his arm. Matthew was always so neat and well-groomed, she thought, and began to wonder if he was unwell. Maybe that's what was wrong.

He started walking slowly towards her. 'I've had something on my mind lately, Paula,' he said in a low, halting voice. 'I've put off talking to you about it, hoping it would go away, but I can see that keeping quiet is only making things worse.'

Paula blanched. There was a sudden sickening feeling in the pit of her stomach. All her carefully rehearsed speeches flew out of her mind. She was suddenly certain he was going to ask for his freedom, and was stunned at how bereft this made her feel.

'What is it, Matthew?' she said at last, unable to keep the tremor out of her voice. She cleared her throat nervously. 'I know that something has been bothering you.'

He threw his jacket over the back of the sofa, loosened his tie, and sat down heavily beside her. Then, slowly, he turned to face her with a grim, determined look.

'I've thought of a hundred ways of leading up to this,' he ground out, 'but now I'm just going to have to spell it out baldly.' He drew in a deep breath. 'I want a family, Paula. I want a child.'

Paula was speechless. For a moment she wasn't sure she'd heard him right. It was not at all what she had expected him to say.

'A child?' she repeated weakly. 'What do you mean? You want us to adopt a baby?' Then a new thought came to her. 'Or do you mean you've found someone you want to marry. . .'

'No, damn it,' he broke in. His face was flushed, and he seemed almost angry. 'I don't want to adopt, and there's no one else. I want *our* child.'

'*Our* child?' She was stunned. 'But that would mean. . .'

'Exactly,' he snapped. He ran a hand over his dark hair. 'I know it sounds crazy, given the terms of our marriage, but I've become obsessed with the idea.' He gave her a pleading look. 'I know it's a lot to ask, given the way you feel about me, about Richard, but would you just think it over, at least consider it?'

Paula's head was spinning. She had to do something, move around, get away from him. She couldn't think straight. She jumped up and walked across the room to the window, and stood staring down at the traffic going by in the street below. She could feel him watching her, waiting for her to say something.

What could she say? It was the last thing she had expected. The implications of his request boggled her mind. Of course, it was out of the question. She couldn't sleep with a man she didn't love, a man who didn't love her.

What would he do if she refused? Would he leave her? Find someone who would accommodate this sudden lust for offspring? She began to grow angry. It was easy enough for him, she thought, clenching her fists at her sides. A man didn't need emotional commitment for sex. Give him a moderately attractive face and body, and it didn't take much to arouse his instincts.

She whirled around, ready to accuse him of merely wanting to use her, when she saw the look on his face. The mouth was set, the grey eyes half-shut, and she knew she was being unfair. Matthew wasn't like that. Although there were aspects of his character she hadn't begun to understand, she did know he was an honourable, considerate man. He liked her, he respected her, and now he wanted her to bear his child.

'You've taken me completely by surprise,' she said at last. 'I had no idea this was what was bothering you.' She smiled weakly. 'I thought you wanted your freedom.'

The heavy dark eyebrows shot up. 'What in the world gave you that idea? I'm perfectly satisfied with our arrangement. I just want a child before I'm too old.'

'Let me think about it for a few days.'

'Of course.' He smiled stiffly. 'I'm grateful you'll go that far.'

It was all she thought about for the next two days. She was tempted, several times, to call Margaret and ask for her advice, but she knew she couldn't do that without revealing to her sister the true nature of her marriage and opening up a torrent of questions and advice.

The one thing she became gradually certain of was that she really did want a child. She thought of suggesting adoption to Matthew, but that could take years, and why adopt when you could have your own?

The unresolved question uppermost in her mind, however, was whether she could go through the necessary preliminaries with Matthew without love, without desire. Certainly, she reasoned, he wasn't repulsive to her. On the contrary, she found him very attractive. She had just never thought of him that way.

She began to look at him with new eyes. He didn't bring up the subject again, and she knew he wouldn't, but the whole atmosphere in the apartment was changed. They treated each other with elaborate courtesy and kept a distance between them, but the tension in the air was electrifying.

By the end of the second day Paula had come to the conclusion that there was no good reason not to do as Matthew wished. After all, she wasn't a blushing young virgin about to be violated for the first time. They were legally married and neither of them were interested in looking for love with anyone else. They would stay together, have a family, make a life. Still she hesitated. What more did she want? Why not just give him what they both wanted?

That second night, before Matthew came home, she went into her bedroom and stood looking down at Richard's photograph. It suddenly dawned on her that she rarely thought about him any more. She would always love him, but the sting of his loss was gone.

She dimly comprehended then why she was still resisting Matthew's request. She was afraid. A wave of sheer terror swept over her when she finally admitted it to herself. To sleep with him, to respond to him physically, would mean not only shutting the door on Richard, but leaving herself emotionally vulnerable to Matthew.

But that was silly. Matthew wasn't asking her for an emotional commitment. Even a physical response on her part wasn't really necessary. She didn't have to show passion, just be available. Surely she could do that for the sake of a child, a child she knew she wanted more and more.

As she reasoned it out, the fear gradually subsided, and she knew what she had to do. She picked up the photograph in its heavy silver frame, walked over to her dresser and opened the bottom drawer where she kept odds and ends of bank statements, old calendars, official documents. She placed the photograph inside and closed the drawer.

Matthew came home late that night. It was after nine before they'd finished eating and Paula had cleared the kitchen. She had made up her mind to give him her answer tonight, and she moved around the kitchen like a robot, putting things away mechanically, her heart pounding dully, painfully in her chest.

When she finally finished in the kitchen, she poured two cups of coffee, set them down on a tray and carried them into the living room. Matthew was sitting on the sofa reading the evening paper.

'Matthew,' she said.

He glanced up at her and smiled. 'Ah, coffee. Just what I need.' He reached for a cup.

She sat down beside him. 'Matthew, I've made up my mind.' His hand stilled in mid-air, then he set the cup carefully back down on the tray and turned to her. 'Yes?'

She nodded. 'I'll do it. I'll have your child.'

There, it was out. She felt weak with relief, and the look of gratitude on his face told her she had done the right thing. For the first time since she'd known him, the pain was gone and the grey eyes were alight with pleasure.

Later that night, Paula stood in her bedroom, gazing at her reflection in the mirror and wondering if Matthew would come to her. After her shower, she had put on a nightgown Margaret had given her as a wedding present.

Her cheeks burned now as she saw how revealing the pale peach-coloured garment was. Thin straps were attached to the points of an extremely low-cut bodice that plunged between her breasts in a deep vee. The material was a paper-thin silk with lace insets at the midriff and sides.

She shook her head. She simply couldn't let him see her like this. She found the loose matching robe, slipped it on and tied it firmly at the neck. But would he even come? Just in case, she turned off the bright overhead light, leaving only a dim lamp burning on the bedside table.

There had been no discussion after she'd given him her answer. The telephone had rung several times, and finally Paula had gone to her room. She wanted to be alone anyway. She *wished* her erratic pulse beat would settle down. It was eleven o'clock by now. Surely he wouldn't come this late. She might as well go to bed.

Then the knock came, and she almost jumped out of her skin. Her heart lurched sickeningly. What was she doing? Was she mad? She couldn't go through with it.

'Paula,' came the low voice. 'May I come in?'

With trembling fingers, she tightened the tie of her robe. 'Come in, Matthew,' she called.

He had brought along a bottle of wine and two glasses, balanced precariously on a tray. When he saw her standing by the dressing table, he only stared for a few seconds, his eyes moving over her, studying her. Burning with embarrassment, she was thankful she'd at least put on the robe over the revealing nightgown.

He was dressed in a dark robe. She could see that his chest was bare and that he had on pyjama bottoms. His hair was still a little damp from the shower, and as he came closer, she noticed that he had shaved. There was a little nick on his chin, and she wondered if he could be a little nervous, too.

When he spoke, however, his voice was steady. 'I thought you might like a glass of wine.' He set the tray down on a corner of the dressing table.

'Yes, please,' she croaked shakily.

He gave her a sharp glance, then poured the wine and handed her a glass. She swallowed it gratefully, and as the warmth spread through her she began to feel a little calmer.

'There's no need to be nervous, Paula,' he said earnestly. 'Trust me. I won't rush you or hurt you.'

She nodded gratefully and looked shyly up at him. She did trust him, and he was far from repulsive to her. The dark robe was belted loosely in front, revealing his strong throat and tanned upper chest. She had never seen him like this before, nor felt his powerful masculinity so intensely.

He reached out a hand and touched her thick dark hair, ran it around to the back of her head, murmuring, 'You're a beautiful woman, Paula.' He pulled her gently towards him. 'I want you to know I am attracted to you. Your hair is like silk. I've wanted to touch it like this so many times.'

His face was so close to hers now that she could see the dark flecks in his silvery eyes, smell the soapy fragrance of his face and hair, and she knew from the light in those hooded eyes that he desired her. She stiffened involuntarily, alarmed at the close contact and the assault on her senses of his close proximity. His hold on her relaxed slightly, and he drew back, looking down into her eyes.

'Don't be afraid, Paula,' he said in a low voice. 'You can back out at any time. Try to relax.'

She nodded her head and swallowed. 'I'll try,' she whispered.

She closed her eyes then and felt his cool lips brush lightly, tentatively against her own. His other hand came up to cup her chin, and when she sighed and leaned against him, she heard him draw in his breath sharply.

His kiss hardened then, and his arms came around her, drawing her closely up against his long, lithe body. He tore his mouth away and placing light, lingering kisses on her face, her eyes, her chin, moved to her ear, his cheek pressed against hers.

'I want you, Paula,' he groaned. 'Put your arms around me. Pretend you love me.'

He wants me, his voice echoed in her ears, and she slowly slid her arms up around his neck. Then his mouth was on hers again, more insistent this time. She felt his tongue move tentatively against her lips, startling her, and she drew back.

'Don't,' he ground out, his lips finding hers again, 'don't leave me like that. Please.'

Her thoughts raced madly. She had made up her mind to go through with this. She couldn't back down now. She had prepared herself to submit passively. What she hadn't been prepared for was the sensations his touch evoked in her. It had never occurred to her that she would respond to him, that her own desire would betray her. She felt herself to be in some kind of danger, but didn't understand why or what it was she feared.

Almost against her will, her lips parted now, and she gasped tremulously as his tongue invaded her mouth. He tasted of toothpaste and the wine he had drunk, a clean heady taste that filled her with pleasure.

His hands were moving now over her back, the thin silky material of her robe sliding sensuously on her bare skin. His touch was firm and sure, and as his warm hands travelled over her ribcage, brushing against the sides of her breasts, she knew she wanted him, too.

He pulled at the ties of her robe and slipped it off her shoulders. One hand came back to settle on her breast, warm and soft, moving sensitively on the bare skin above the low bodice of the wispy nightgown. She gasped as she felt his fingers playing lightly with the barely covered nipple, taut and thrusting under the thin silk.

All thinking ceased when he slipped the thin straps of her gown from her shoulders and the hand moved from one aroused, quivering breast to the other. She threw her head back when his mouth left hers and travelled down her neck to her collarbone, to her breast, leaving a trail of fire until it closed moistly on one hard peak.

She hadn't known, hadn't dreamed, lovemaking could be like this. Her whole body was a mass of sensation. All she was aware of were Matthew's hands and mouth on her body, his ragged breathing. The frantic potency of his unleashed passion overwhelmed her. Gone were the iron control and the remote manner, to reveal a Matthew she had never known existed.

When he released her momentarily to shrug out of his own robe, she clutched blindly at him, her hands roaming over the smooth bare chest, the hard muscles of his arms and shoulders, and when he came back to her, crushing her to him, she moaned deep in her throat and moulded her body to his with a wild longing she had never experienced before.

His hands slid down to her hips, pulling her lower body against his, his need for her unmistakable, sure proof of her power over him. She looked up into his eyes. In the dim light burning across the room by the side of the bed, she could see the fire in the grey eyes and the broad chest heaving as he struggled for control.

'Now, Paula,' he muttered in a rasping breath. 'Now.'

She nodded. 'Yes, Matthew. Oh, yes.'

Slowly, his arms still tight around her, he began to propel her backward towards the bed, his strong thighs guiding her steps as if in a dance. He lowered her gently down onto the bed, then reached out to turn off the light with one hand, removing the pyjama bottoms at the same time with the other.

The darkness only seemed to intensify their passion. Paula clung to him as his body covered hers, and then they were finally joined together, the pounding momentum building to a crescendo of pure, soul-shattering pleasure, as she became Matthew's wife at last.

Paula woke up in the middle of the night, her whole body still tingling from Matthew's passionate lovemaking. She had fallen asleep in his arms, and as memory came back to her, renewed desire came with it. She stretched contentedly, a little smile on her face, and turned to reach out for him.

The other side of the bed was empty. He had gone. With a sharp pang of disappointment, Paula rolled back on to her pillow and stared into the darkness.

Why had he left her? Hadn't she pleased him? Perhaps she had appeared too eager. Her cheeks burned as she recalled the wild abandon with which she had responded to his lovemaking. She sat up in bed and suddenly realised she was still naked.

She sank back down with a groan. What had got into her? Matthew must be disgusted with her. She tried to form a mental image of him as he had appeared to her earlier tonight, aroused, splendid in his naked masculinity, the grey eyes blazing with desire, the warm hands and mouth worshipping her body, her husband in every sense of the word.

But all she could envision now that he was gone was the cool remote stranger she shared an apartment with. Was tonight, the intense physical passion they had shared, only a dream? No, she thought, vividly aware that her mouth and breasts were still sore from his violent lovemaking. Richard had never made love to her like that, and the experience was unforgettable.

Oh, why did he leave me, she groaned. She switched on the lamp and got out of bed to retrieve her nightgown, still lying on the floor by the dressing table where Matthew had removed it earlier. She slipped it on and glanced into the mirror. As she stared at her passion-drugged reflection, recalling again his kiss, his touch, his naked desire, it slowly began to dawn on her why she had been so afraid of a physical relationship with him.

I'm falling in love with him, she thought with a gasp of horror. How else could she explain her mindless response, her thrill of pleasure at the desire she had evoked in him?

She sank down on to the padded stool and covered her face with her hands. Before tonight, she knew she had liked him, enjoyed being with him, admired and respected him. All it took was the recognition of her physical desire for him to push her to the brink of love.

How could I have been so blind? she agonised. The fear, the hesitation, the doubts of the last few days had stemmed from an instinctive need to protect herself against this very thing. She gazed bleakly at her reflection in the mirror, thinking over their night together.

The stark fact was that even though Matthew quite obviously felt desire for her, not one word of love had passed his lips. He had no intention of falling in love with her. He was still under the powerful spell of the beautiful, elusive Beth.

Matthew wanted a child, she concluded at last, but he didn't want a wife.

Paula got up late the next morning. She had gone back to bed in the middle of the night and finally fallen into a fitful sleep. Matthew had already gone. He'd made his own breakfast and left his dishes piled neatly in the kitchen sink.

As she moved mechanically through the day, doing what had to be done, Paula clung to the frail hope that she might have been mistaken about Matthew's feelings for her, the reason he had left her last night. He was a considerate man, sensitive to the needs of others. Perhaps he hadn't wanted to embarrass her by his presence in her bed first thing in the morning.

In the clear light of day, the whole thing didn't seem quite as bad as it had in the middle of the night. By late afternoon, she was even feeling a little cheerful. She loved her husband. What was so terrible about that? There was still the chance that he might learn to love her, too.

She was in the kitchen preparing dinner when she heard his key in the lock. Her whole body went rigid. As his footsteps came closer, she tried to busy herself at the sink, her back to the door. She wanted to appear as casual as possible, but her heart was thudding so hard and her fingers trembling so uncontrollably, she was afraid she'd drop the dishes she was rinsing.

She could sense him standing at the doorway behind her for some moments before he spoke. She couldn't have turned around and looked at him to save her life. She knew her face was flaming.

'How are you, Paula?' he said at last.

'Oh, I'm fine, just fine,' she replied brightly, still unable to face him. Blindly, she turned on the water tap, just for something to do, and immediately scalded her hand in the sudden burst of hot water.

She gave a little cry, more of annoyance at herself than of pain, and shut the water off. He was beside her now, looking down at the hand, which was reddening and beginning to blister.

'You don't seem fine,' he said drily. He reached out and turned on the cold water, then took her hand and placed it under the cooling stream. 'Is that better?' he asked.

She nodded, still unable to speak. He turned the water off and reached for a towel. Gravely, gently, he began to dry her hand.

'It's much better, now, thanks,' she muttered. 'It was a stupid thing to do.' His touch unnerved her.

'Look at me, Paula,' he said at last, tossing the towel over a chair. He put his hand under her chin and forced her head up so that she had to face him. 'Now, let's start over again. How are you?'

The grey eyes were kind, and she recognised genuine concern in the deep voice. She smiled weakly. 'I'm fine. Really.'

He raised one dark eyebrow and held her gaze in his. 'No regrets? About last night?'

She shook her head slowly, melting under the silvery gaze. He needed a shave, she thought, and longed to run her hand up over the light stubble on the flat, hard cheeks. 'No. No regrets.'

He smiled then and leaned down to kiss her lightly on the nose. 'Good girl.' His hand dropped away then, and he turned to go. 'I have a meeting tonight,' he called over his shoulder. 'Do I have time to shower?'

'Yes. Yes, of course. It's so warm I've just fixed a cold supper. It can be ready any time.'

Then he was gone.

She waited up for him that night until past eleven o'clock, staring blindly at the television set, watching whatever programme came on without paying any attention to it.

She didn't know what to do, what to think. Their conversation over dinner had been desultory and impersonal. Matthew had been appointed to an important Senate subcommittee, and that seemed to be all he had on his mind. She had listened to him, waiting for some personal word, a touch, even a glance, but when he had finished his dinner, he had gone off to his meeting with only a casual good night.

She finally switched off the television and went to bed. Lying there, listening for him, she thought over his strange manner to her. What was going through his mind? Did he regret coming to her last night, revealing his naked passion to her?

At dinner she had found herself looking at him with new eyes. She'd always known he was an attractive man, but now his cool good looks had an entirely new effect on her. As she watched him eat or speak, all she could think of was that fine sensitive mouth on hers. When his hands reached out for a cup or a fork, she stared at the long fingers and remembered how they had felt moving on her body.

Finally, just as she was drifting off to sleep, she heard him come in the front door, his step in the hall. She sat bolt upright in bed, her heart pounding. She could sense his presence just outside her door, hesitating, listening. Should she call out to him? Before she could make up her mind, she heard the soft footsteps moving away down the hall towards his own bedroom.

The next day they only saw each other briefly at breakfast. He called her in the middle of the day to say he wouldn't be home for dinner. Paula had known when she married him that a senator's life was taken up with time-consuming obligations. Then, it hadn't seemed to matter. Now, it was an agony.

That night she left her light on after she went to bed, thinking he might come if he knew she was still awake. She read in bed until midnight, then dozed off. When she woke up, the light was still burning and it was after two. If he had come home, he either hadn't knocked at her door or she had been asleep and hadn't heard him.

The next night they went out together to a cocktail party, then on to dinner at a restaurant with several other people. Matthew treated her with the same cool courtesy and polite deference he always had, but even when they were alone, on the way home, their conversation was impersonal. She noticed that not once during the evening had he touched her.

By now, Paula had had enough. She had slept badly the last two nights and was so absorbed in trying to figure out what was going on in her husband's head that she couldn't work, couldn't even eat properly. Did he think that one visit was going to produce a pregnancy? Was that all he wanted from her? Did he see her only as some kind of brood mare, her only value in his eyes as a receptacle for his offspring?

By the time they got home late that night, she had worked herself into a fine self-righteous anger, and as soon as they were inside the apartment she stalked off to her own room, tossing a brief 'Good night' at him over her shoulder. She didn't even turn around.

Still simmering with resentment, she threw her clothes off, put on her old cotton nightgown, turned out the light and flopped into bed. If there had been a lock on the door, she would have turned it. She fell asleep immediately, exhausted from the nervous intensity of the last two days, the sleepless nights.

She dreamed that Matthew had come to her at last, so vividly that she could feel his face next to hers, his hand moving on her breast. Then, gradually awakening, she realised it wasn't a dream.

Her eyelids fluttered, opened, and focused on a dim form sitting on the edge of the bed, leaning over her. His mouth was at her ear.

'Is it all right if I stay, Paula?'

She tried to recall her earlier anger, but the soft quick breath in her ear, the gentle fingertips tracing a line across the low bodice of her nightgown, distracted her. She murmured her assent, still dazed from the short sleep, and felt him slip into bed beside her.

When his arms came around her and she reached out for him, her hands fell on bare flesh, and she realised he was naked. She drew in her breath sharply, and then his mouth came down on hers, blotting out all thought, reducing her to a quivering, yielding response.

His lovemaking was more tender tonight, his kisses more seductive, his touch gentler. When she sat up so that he could pull the nightgown over her head, his hands slid back down lingeringly over her upraised arms, her shoulders, stopped briefly to cup and mould her warm breasts, then moved down over her flat stomach, to her thighs, the soles of her feet and back up again.

Paula found herself responding as powerfully to this sensuous gentleness as she had to his wilder passion. She had to bite her lip several times to stop herself from telling him she loved him, intuition warning her that such a declaration at this point would ruin everything between them.

She knew he didn't love her with his mind or his heart. But her deepest feminine instinct assured her that he did indeed love her with his hands, his mouth, his body and in time he might learn to love her as fully as she loved him. She could hope, anyway.

Once again, he left her after she had fallen asleep in his arms. When she awoke the next morning and found that he was gone, her hopes vanished and the bitterness returned. She lay for a

long time alone in bed staring up at the ceiling,
wondering what to do.

What could she do? She had to accept the fact
that to Matthew she was only an object of desire,
good merely for satisfying his lust, bearing his
children. Could she live with that? The future
yawned emptily before her, frightening her.

CHAPTER SEVEN

MARGARET and William were coming to dinner the next night. The timing was bad, Paula thought, as she laboured all day over a complicated French ragoût. Not only was the situation with Matthew unsettling, preoccupying, but she had just been given a new commission for some fashion illustrations from an exclusive shop in Philadelphia that had a deadline in two weeks, and couldn't seem to concentrate on it.

By the time Matthew got home that evening, she was a wreck. The ragoût was tasteless, the consommé wouldn't clarify and the chocolate torte layers sagged ominously in the middle when she took them out of the oven. It was six o'clock, she hadn't dressed yet, and when Matthew strolled into the kitchen she was near tears.

'Something smells good,' he said pleasantly.

She brushed the heavy fringe of smooth black hair away from her damp forehead and eyed the caved-in torte with dismay. The kitchen was like an oven. What had got into her, she wondered, to tackle a heavy French menu in the middle of July?

She turned and glared at Matthew. Somehow the sight of him standing there at the doorway, so cool and neat in his lightweight tan trousers and short-sleeved white dress shirt infuriated her, and she vented all her anger and frustration on him.

'Well, that's good,' she snapped, 'because the dinner is ruined.'

He only raised his dark eyebrows and walked

slowly to her side, looking down at the offending cake layers lying on the draining board. His close proximity only upset her further. The jacket of his suit was slung casually over one shoulder, hooked into his thumb, and his bare forearm brushed lightly against hers as he reached out to pick up a few crumbs.

'Chocolate,' he murmured appreciatively. 'My favourite. It tastes good. What's wrong with it?'

'What's wrong with it?' she cried, pointing. 'Just take a look at it!'

He did so, then murmured, 'I gather it's not supposed to, um, droop like that in the middle.'

She could tell he was trying hard not to laugh, and this only infuriated her even more. 'It's not funny,' she snapped.

It made her uncomfortable to have him standing so close to her. If we were really married, she grumbled to herself, I could turn to him for comfort, cry on his shoulder, and we could even laugh about it. What's a ruined dinner when you're in love?

But we aren't in love, she thought glumly as she turned to the stove and stared down at the pan of consommé simmering there, still clouded and muddy. We only sleep together once in a while. Her eyes burned with tears of self-pity, which finally began to spill over.

'Hey, Paula,' he called to her softly now. 'It's not worth crying over. After all, it's only William and Margaret, not Mr and Mrs President. They won't care.'

'I know,' she sniffed, trying to muffle her childish tears.

His arm came around her then, pulling her towards him. At this unexpected sign of affection, the dam burst, and she turned and sobbed wetly into his chest, soaking the white shirt with her tears.

As the outburst subsided, she began to feel better. What difference did a silly dinner make when Matthew was there to hold her, to comfort her? She longed to stay in the shelter of his strong arm forever, forget the dinner, forget William and Margaret, forget the whole world.

His hand was moving in a gentle soothing motion over her bare arm, and as she quieted down, the movement began to lull her into a mindless enjoyment of his touch. Her pulses started to race as the pressure of his hand increased, became less comforting, more sensuous.

He could feel it, too, she knew, as she listened to his own heartbeat quicken under her ear. His fingers moved up under the short sleeve of her cotton shirt, on to her bare shoulder, and she leaned closer to him, pressing herself against him.

She raised her head slightly so that she could look up at him through eyelashes still wet with tears. His face was grave, his mouth set in a hard line, but the grey eyes gleamed with something she recognised instantly, unmistakably as desire.

As their eyes met, the hand on her shoulder stilled. She watched transfixed, as the dark head bent fractionally, haltingly, down towards her, and closed her eyes, waiting for his kiss, longing for the touch of his mouth on hers. Suddenly, she felt his hand tighten painfully. His whole body stiffened away from her, and she thought she heard him swear softly under his breath.

Her eyes flew open. He was looking at her now with something like hatred, his eyes narrowed and cold. Then he dropped his hand from her shoulder. She shrank back, confused and embarrassed.

His jacket had dropped to the floor while he had held her for those few moments. He leaned over now to retrieve it, and when he straightened up again, the pleasant remote mask had reappeared on his face and he smiled distantly.

'Feeling better?' She nodded and turned her head away to hide her dismay at this sudden change in him. 'That's good,' he said calmly. 'It'll be all right. You'll see. I'll go shower and dress now.'

'Yes,' she said dully, still unable to face him. 'They'll be here at seven-thirty. I still have to get ready myself.'

She heard his footsteps as he walked out of the kitchen. When he was gone, she stood at the stove for several moments mindlessly stirring the consommé, trying to collect her thoughts, trying to understand the reason for Matthew's abrupt withdrawal just when he had been about to kiss her.

She sighed deeply, frowned at the consommé, and went down the hall to her bedroom. In one way, she thought as she showered, the episode gave her hope. His response to her in the kitchen had been spontaneous, not a planned event. He had wanted *her*, Paula, not merely the use of her body for the purpose of creating a child.

She *knew* he had wanted to kiss her, had fully intended to kiss her. Why had he stopped? After drying herself, she sat down at the dressing table brushing her short dark hair vigorously, staring into the mirror, pondering. Of course, she had looked a mess, teary-eyed, hot, dishevelled. Was that it?

No, she thought, as she slipped on a short white sundress and zipped it up the back. Her appearance hadn't stopped him when he initiated the embrace. What then? Was he afraid of rejection? Of course not! Not only could a man like Matthew Stratton handle rejection quite easily, but her response to him had been unmistakable.

Of course, she knew the real reason. It was Beth. She had to face it. As her own grief over Richard's death had faded, she had automatically assumed, had hoped, that Matthew was also recovering from Beth. Now she knew better. Even though Matthew wanted her physically, he was still hopelessly in love with his dead wife, would always be caught in her spell. How could she fight a dead woman? Beth lived on in his heart as a beautiful, unattainable dream.

He sleeps with me, Paula thought bitterly as she slashed a touch of pale coral lipstick on her mouth, but he'll never love me. He'll never allow himself to. How can he when he's enchanted by a ghost?

It had been a terrible mistake to sleep with him, to allow herself to respond to him physically. Somehow she would have to see to it that it never happened again. She simply must harden her heart against him, refuse him her body. Otherwise she would be lost.

Miraculously, the dinner was not the disaster Paula had feared. At the last minute, she had strained the consommé through a cheesecloth, piled whipped cream into the fallen centre of the torte, and reseasoned the ragoût before William and Margaret arrived.

By the time they sat down to a candlelit dinner

out on the balcony, a slight breeze had sprung up, cooling the hot, humid air, and when they had finished the meal, Paula was feeling more like herself again, buoyed up by her resolution to resist Matthew with every weapon at her command. She could do it. She wasn't a gullible young girl, nor so far gone that she wouldn't get over him in time.

She tried to look at him now, sitting across the table from her, with more detachment. He was unattainable, she told herself, steeling herself against him when he smiled at her or spoke to her. He didn't even exist, as far as a real relationship was concerned. She could even return his smile coolly, speak to him, without giving way to any warm feeling for him. It was an effort now—he was even more attractive and appealing—but with practice it would get easier.

'That was a fine dinner, Paula,' William was saying now over brandy. 'I didn't know you had it in you.'

'Yes,' Margaret agreed. 'The torte was especially delicious. You must give me the recipe.'

William turned to Matthew, who was leaning back in his chair smoking a long thin cigar, apparently totally relaxed and unaware of any change in Paula's manner toward him.

'When will you be going on that fact-finding mission to Palestine, Matthew?'

'How did you know about that? It's supposed to be a secret. I haven't even told Paula.'

William chuckled. 'Oh, very little escapes the notice of the President's staff. Actually, I only know the bare outline. What can you tell me about it?'

Matthew shrugged and took a sip of brandy. He

was thinking over his response carefully, Paula knew, watching him. He looks so handsome tonight, she thought, in his dark suit, the candlelight flickering over his fine tanned features. Then she caught herself, remembering her resolve, and tore her eyes away.

'I guess there's no harm in discussing it now,' he said at last, 'since we're leaving in a few days.' He shot Paula an apologetic look when he saw the startled expression on her face. 'Sorry, Paula. Even wives had to be kept in the dark.'

Wives! she thought disgustedly. He makes it sound as though we had a real marriage, as though such concealment would matter.

'Of course,' she murmured coolly, giving nothing of her feelings away.

He went on to explain the mission, which would include the members of his Senate subcommittee, two men high up in the State Department and several Congressmen. Paula didn't even listen to him, except to hear that he'd be gone for two weeks.

Good, she thought. I want him out of here. A separation is just what I need at this point. It will give me time to get him out of my system. And when he comes back, I'll tell him he can either look for another brood mare or adopt a child, because I'm never going to let him in my bed again.

Her righteous indignation gave her strength. She could watch him now, listen to him speaking, and feel all affection for him ebbing away as she hardened herself against him.

'You're looking well, Paula,' Margaret said in a low voice. 'Married life seems to suit you.'

Paula turned to her and smiled. 'Yes, it does.

I'm quite content.' And she would be, she vowed, as soon as she got Matthew out of her heart for good.

Margaret nodded with satisfaction. 'I thought you would be.' She glanced down the table at Matthew, who was listening attentively to William, a serious expression on his face. 'You're very lucky, you know. Matthew is a fine man. You're the envy of every unattached woman in Washington.'

Paula kept smiling. If her sister and all those women only knew, she thought bitterly, just what kind of husband Matthew Stratton was, they'd change their tune.

It was midnight before William and Margaret left. Paula was exhausted, physically and emotionally, from the long afternoon spent slaving in the kitchen, the shock of grasping Matthew's real feelings at last, and the ordeal of sustaining a carefree charade for her sister's benefit.

When the door finally shut behind them, she heaved a deep sigh of relief. The muscles of her face were rigid from smiling, and she had a splitting headache. She longed for bed, but decided to clean up the dinner debris tonight, as much to keep a distance from Matthew as to get it out of the way so she wouldn't have to face it in the morning.

She began to clear off the table on the balcony, piling dishes, silver and glassware on a large tray. Matthew came to the door and stood there watching her. She couldn't look at him, not yet, and she bustled about busily, making a loud clatter.

'What can I do to help?' he asked.

'Nothing,' she replied briefly without looking at him. 'You might as well go on to bed.'

He was silent, but made no move to leave. When the tray was piled as high as possible, Paula picked it up. A glass tipped over and a stack of cups wobbled precariously.

'Here,' Matthew said, striding towards her and taking the tray from her. 'Let me do that.'

Wordlessly, she relinquished the tray and followed him into the kitchen. He set the tray down on the counter and turned to her. She brushed past him, turned on the tap and started rinsing dishes.

'I'm sorry I couldn't tell you about the Palestine trip,' he said after a long silence.

'No need to apologise,' she said over her shoulder. 'I understand perfectly.'

She turned off the water and leaned over to stack the china and silverware into the dishwasher. She wished he'd just leave. Why was he still hanging around? Most of the men she knew seemed to vanish miraculously when there was kitchen work to be done.

'What's wrong, then?' he asked quietly. 'I thought. . .'

She shot him a quick look and even managed to force an insincere smile. 'Nothing's wrong,' she replied briskly. 'I have a little headache.' What had he thought? That she would fall into his arms?

'Would you like to come with me? To Palestine? Some of the wives are going along.'

She straightened up and slowly dried her hands on a towel. For one brief moment she was tempted. Perhaps if they got clear away from Washington, the whole country, he'd forget Beth and turn to her. Two weeks alone with him might make all the difference.

Then she remembered the deadline on her new

commission. She'd give it up in a minute if he really wanted her to go. She looked at him.

'I don't see how I can,' she said slowly. 'I have to get those drawings in for the Philadelphia store in two weeks.' If he asks me again to go, I will, she thought, and the hell with the new commission.

She watched him carefully, trying to read his thoughts. He seemed to be debating within himself, and she held her breath. Then she saw him frown and look away.

'Of course,' he said. 'I forgot about that.' He gave her a wintry smile. 'If you're all through here, why don't you turn in. I think I will.' He started towards the door. 'Be sure and take something for that headache,' he said. Then he was gone.

For the next two days they hardly saw each other. Matthew was deeply involved in meetings and briefing sessions for his trip to Palestine, and only came home to fall, exhausted, into his own bed.

In a way, it was a relief to Paula not to have to see him or talk to him. Every indication was that he only regretted the few instances when he had seemed to warm towards her, and she was determined to put up the old barriers again.

She plunged immediately into her new job, even before he left, and found once again that work was the most effective antidote to pain. Each day without him only confirmed her decision to put an end to the physical side of their relationship. She didn't know how she would tell him, or what would remain of their marriage when she did, but she knew she had to do it.

Matthew had been gone a week when Margaret called her late Friday afternoon to ask her to come out to the house in Virginia for the weekend.

'Oh, I can't, Margaret,' she said. 'I'm in the middle of these new illustrations and can't leave them. I'll be lucky to meet the deadline as it is.'

'Well, come for the day, then,' Margaret insisted. 'One day can't make that much difference.'

But Paula was firm. With her marriage most likely in ruins, she'd need her work more than ever. 'No. Not even a day.'

Margaret heaved a deep sigh. 'Oh, very well, have it your way. It beats me how anyone so meek can be so stubborn. Have lunch with me Monday at any rate.'

'All right,' Paula agreed quickly, glad she had won so easily. 'Stop by the apartment around noon.'

After she hung up the telephone, she stood by the hall table deep in thought. What did Margaret mean, saying she was 'meek'? It made her sound weak. And why was she so insistent on seeing her? Ever since her marriage to Matthew, Margaret had given up the constant surveillance of her activities and appeared to have gone on to new and greater challenges.

She obviously had something on her mind, and, knowing Margaret, it wouldn't be pleasant.

On Monday, as soon as they had settled themselves in the sedate, old-fashioned restaurant, Margaret came right to the point. Her choice of a place to have lunch, out of the way and quiet, only confirmed Paula's suspicion that she had more on her mind than a casual sisterly meeting.

'I suppose you know,' Margaret began when they had ordered, 'that Michele Lathrop's father is on Matthew's mission to Palestine and that she went with him.'

Paula hadn't known, and she couldn't hide the look of stunned surprise on her face as she looked into Margaret's probing, narrowed eyes. Then she thought quickly, what difference does it make to me?

'No,' she said, recovering herself, 'I didn't know. Is there some significance to that fact?'

Margaret snorted and leaned back in her chair. 'I wouldn't even trust *William* with that man-eater,' she announced, 'and no one is safer than William. He doesn't even like blondes.'

Paula reddened, suddenly angry. 'If you're implying that Matthew and Michele. . .'

Margaret held up a hand. 'I'm not implying anything,' she cut in. 'I'm only saying you're a fool not to have gone with him. Why tempt fate? Didn't he ask you to go?'

'Well, yes, he did,' Paula faltered, 'but I couldn't. I have this new job.'

'Oh, *damn* your job!' Margaret cried in exasperation. She leaned across the table and lowered her voice to a hiss. 'Your precious job will be cold comfort if you lose your husband over it.'

Paula forced a weak smile. 'If I should lose my husband, Margaret, I'll need my job more than ever.'

Margaret opened her mouth to deliver a stinging retort when the waiter appeared with their lunch. When he was gone they ate silently for a while. Paula was glad of the respite, and the chance to mull over Margaret's disturbing news.

Actually, she reasoned, she had nothing to fear from Michele Lathrop, given the conditions of her marriage to Matthew. She supposed it was quite possible he might have an affair with her, but she wasn't worried about Michele. She could have fought Michele. Her real rival was Beth, and she had already resigned herself to the fact that she couldn't compete with a ghostly illusion for Matthew's love.

'Well?' Margaret said at last. 'What are you going to do about it?'

Paula continued to eat her lunch. 'I'm not going to do anything about it,' she replied calmly between bites. 'I'm not worried about Matthew.'

Margaret raised her well-groomed eyebrows in supplication. 'Oh, you poor innocent ninny!' she exclaimed. 'If I were you. . .'

'You're not me, Margaret,' Paula broke in firmly. She carefully laid down her fork on her plate, barely able to contain her anger. 'You know nothing about my marriage to Matthew. Nothing! Now, if you can't stay off the subject, perhaps we'd better leave, because I *will not* discuss it any more.'

Margaret goggled at her, open-mouthed for several seconds. Then, accepting defeat gracefully, she put on a hurt look and continued eating her lunch.

'No need to get huffy, darling. Let's just forget it,' and she immediately went on to impart the latest tidbit of Washington gossip.

In the days that followed Paula tried to put that conversation with Margaret out of her mind. What did she care what Matthew did with Michele Lathrop or anyone else? He had said before their marriage that he didn't intend to have affairs or to embarrass her publicly. If he's changed his mind, it didn't make any difference to her.

Still, at odd moments during that last week before he was due home, Paula couldn't avoid the image of Matthew and Michele together. She remembered the first night they met, when he had been with Michele, and the way the lovely blonde had plastered herself up against him when they danced.

Was that firm mouth kissing Michele, now? she wondered in an agony of jealous frustration. Were those long fingers trailing over her body? She was astounded at the intensity of her reaction even to the possibility of such an occurrence, and convinced herself at last that this was all the more reason to put a stop to their physical life before she was truly lost.

She would tell him as soon as he got back, she decided, so they could start out on a clean slate, and during the several days left before his return, she rehearsed over and over again in her mind what she would say. She wanted to be kind, but firm. She *had* to be firm.

He arrived back the following Sunday, exhausted but exhilarated with the success of the mission.

'I think we've made a real breakthrough in our negotiations between the Palestinians and Israelis,' he told her that first night over dinner.

She had been so glad to see him when he came home that she had almost forgotten her resentment and the resolution she had made to put an end to their physical relationship. And he had been glad to see her, too, she knew. His eyes had lit up when she greeted him at the door, and he had leaned down impulsively and kissed her briefly on the mouth.

Watching him now across the table from her, telling her about his trip, she found herself wishing once again with all her heart that he was really her husband. He looked tired, but tanned and fit, as though he had been outdoors a great deal in the past two weeks.

He had showered and shaved as soon as he got home, grimy and dishevelled from the long airplane trip, and was dressed now in a dark blue knit shirt, open at the neck. She couldn't keep her eyes off the strong forearms, the large sensitive hands, the fine mouth and long column of his throat as he ate or spoke to her or gestured to make a point.

They had coffee after dinner out on the balcony. It was after nine by the time they'd finished dinner, and the sun had just set. In the warm dusky August twilight, he looked more handsome than ever, and Paula began to change her mind about the talk she had planned to have with him, her decision not to have his child after all.

'How about you?' he asked, turning to her. 'Did you finish your illustrations on time?'

'Yes, I did. The store seemed to like them and have given me another commission for their Christmas catalogue.'

'Wonderful.' He paused. 'Still, I wish you'd come with me, Paula. I missed you.'

She looked at him, her heart leaping in her breast. He had missed her! What did that mean? She thought about the beautiful Michele Lathrop, so convenient, so handy. Had he missed her enough to turn to the seductive blonde?

'With Michele Lathrop along, I wouldn't think any of the men would have missed their wives,' she said lightly, playfully.

He gave her an odd, appraising look, then threw back his head and laughed. 'You're not jealous, are you, Paula?'

His amusement angered her. 'Of course not,' she retorted. 'At least not of Michele.'

Sensing her irritation, he sobered. 'What do you mean by that? I told you before we married that I would never embarrass you. I meant it.'

She stood up and began to collect the coffee cups, avoiding his eyes. 'It really doesn't matter, Matthew,' she said airily. 'We hardly have the kind of marriage where jealousy or fidelity have any meaning.'

As she passed by him on her way to the kitchen, he reached out and took her firmly by the arm. Her skin quivered at the unexpected touch, as though a charge of electricity had passed from his hand to her arm, and she almost dropped the cups. She looked down at him, wide-eyed and tense.

He was frowning, a puzzled look in the grey eyes. 'What makes you say a thing like that?' he asked. 'After what's passed between us, how can you say that fidelity has no meaning?'

Their eyes were locked together. Paula's mind raced. What was he saying? Was it possible he did care for her after all? For one wild moment, her heart began to sing. She opened her mouth to speak.

Then the telephone rang shrilly. Matthew released her arm and jumped to his feet. 'Hell,' he muttered. 'That's Martin. I said I'd call him as soon as I got back, and I forgot.'

He went into the front hall to answer the telephone, and Paula took the cups on into the kitchen, hope rising within her. Maybe it was going to be all right. Maybe Beth's spell was finally broken.

While she busied herself straightening up the kitchen, she could hear him speaking on the telephone in a low voice for several minutes. Suddenly he called to her. She went into the hall. His hand was over the mouthpiece.

'Paula, would you mind going into my bedroom and getting my notebook out of my suitcase,' he said in an urgent tone. 'It's black leather and should be right on top. All my figures are in it.'

'Of course,' she said, and hurried off down the hall.

When she entered his room and glanced around in search of his suitcase, the first thing she noticed was that the photograph of Beth in its silver frame was gone from the bedside table. Her heart gave a great leap. Had he put it away, as she had Richard's? She almost laughed aloud with relief and joy.

Then she saw the open suitcase on the floor beside the bed, the notebook right on top. What a neat packer Matthew is, she thought, as she picked up the black notebook and saw the neatly folded shirts beneath it.

Then her eye was caught by a shiny edge of metal, just visible below the stack of shirts. She stood for a second staring, a sudden sickening wave of apprehension sweeping through her. She lifted up the shirts. It was as she had feared. Beth's lovely face smiled up at her.

She turned and hurried back to Matthew, thrust the notebook at him and went back into the kitchen. So much for hope, she thought bitterly, as she stood at the window staring blankly out into the dark night. He had taken Beth's photograph with him. He couldn't bear to be parted from that last remnant of his dead wife—his only wife, Paula knew now—for two weeks.

She could have fought a woman like Michele

Lathrop and won, she thought fiercely, her hands gripping the edge of the counter. Trying to fight Beth was a losing battle. She—or her image of perfection—was so firmly entrenched in Matthew's heart and mind as a wifely paragon that it was hopeless, a totally lost cause.

When she heard him say goodbye and hang up at last, she went into the living room, determined now to have it out with him before she weakened again. She simply could not bear to have him touch her now, knowing she was only a surrogate for the woman he really wanted.

He was still standing by the telephone, leafing through the notebook. When he saw her, he smiled and started walking towards her. For a second she wavered, then, her fists clenched at her sides, her chin raised, she decided that bluntness was her only recourse.

'There's something I must say to you, Matthew,' she said in a firm tone. 'I've been doing a lot of thinking since you've been gone, and I've decided that I'm not satisfied with the way our arrangement is going.'

He gave her a puzzled look. 'I don't understand. I thought. . .'

'I've decided I don't want a child,' she blurted out.

There was a tense silence then. He continued to stand motionless before her, his face blank.

'What you mean,' he said at last in a hard, grinding tone, 'is that you don't want me in your bed.'

She jerked her head back as though he had struck her. 'Very well, if you want to put it that way,' she said stiffly. Oh, God, she thought, this was agony. He was looking at her now as though he hated her.

He took a step towards her, his attitude faintly threatening, and glared down at her. 'You lie!' he growled angrily, his face dark and forbidding. His hands gripped her by the shoulders, and he shook her a little. 'If you're trying to tell me you don't want me, don't respond to me, you're lying.'

Paula could only stand there, rigid with shock, appalled at his fury. She had never seen Matthew angry before. The grey eyes blazed, his mouth was curled in a sneer of contempt and his strong fingers bit painfully into her shoulders.

'You're hurting me,' she whispered at last.

He pushed her from him so suddenly then that she stumbled backwards, almost losing her balance. With a muttered curse, his hands left her and he turned away, his dark head bowed, his shoulders heaving as he struggled for control.

Still in a state of shock, Paula tried to gather her wits. She had expected him to be mildly disappointed, but his violent reaction stunned her to the core of her being. It was as though the Matthew she knew was gone, and a dangerous stranger had suddenly taken his place.

'Matthew,' she began hesitantly. When he didn't answer, she raised her voice. She had to reach him, make him understand. 'Matthew, you told me that first night that I could back out at any time. That's all I'm doing.'

He turned to face her, still wild-eyed, but apparently having gained control of himself. 'Why?' he ground out. 'Why are you backing out now? It's too late.'

She lowered her eyes. 'I have to. It's—it's become too painful for me.'

'What is it that's so painful for you, Paula?' he growled mockingly. 'Sleeping with me? You didn't act as though you were in pain. On the contrary, I'd say you enjoyed every minute of it.'

She coloured deeply and muttered, 'That's not fair. I admit I responded physically to you, but. . .' She hesitated, unable to go on. She couldn't tell him she loved him, not now, not when he was glaring at her that way, the twisted features full of contempt.

'Well, then? What is it?' he demanded. When she didn't reply, he lowered his voice and asked in a soft, menacing tone, 'Is it because I'm not Richard?'

Her head came up then and her green eyes blazed at him. 'How dare you say such a thing to me!' She was so angry she could hardly speak. He was the one who couldn't even be parted from his dead wife's photograph for two weeks. 'You, of all people!'

He coloured deeply then, and his shoulders slumped, as though all the anger had suddenly drained out of him. He passed a hand over his dark hair and took several deep breaths. Then he looked at her again.

'You're right, of course,' he said, his voice toneless, devoid of emotion. 'I'm sorry, Paula. I don't know what came over me.' He shrugged and gave her a wry, apologetic smile. 'It's just that I really did miss you and looked forward to being with you again. When you hit me with this sudden decision of yours, it simply took my breath away. I had no idea. . .'

Her heart went out to him. She *had* sprung it on him rather brutally. She had been piqued by the sight of that photograph in his suitcase just when she was beginning to hope again that he might love her.

'Matthew, I'm very fond of you. And I have to admit that I did respond to you. I guess I have all the instincts of a normal woman, and you're an attractive man. But, don't you see?' She spread her arms wide in a helpless gesture. 'For me, sex without love is a mockery, a travesty, a betrayal of my deepest beliefs. I think it's *because* I responded to you that I have to put a stop to it.'

'That doesn't make any sense.'

She shrugged. 'No, to a man I don't suppose it would.' She lifted her chin. 'At any rate, my mind is made up. If you want your freedom, of course I won't put any obstacles in your way.'

He stared glumly at her for a full minute. 'Let me think about it,' he said at last. 'Right now I don't know what I want.'

CHAPTER EIGHT

THE next morning at breakfast Matthew apologised for his behaviour the night before. He looked haggard and worn, his face drawn, the lines around his eyes deeper, as though he had passed a sleepless night.

'I don't know what got into me,' he said just as he was leaving the table. He smiled down at her bleakly. 'You'll have to admit I usually am able to exercise more control over my emotions.'

Paula sat and stared down at her plate. As was her habit, she had appeared at the breakfast table fully dressed and was wearing a tailored cotton shirtwaist dress, her short dark hair neatly combed, a dash of pale lipstick on her mouth. She and Matthew had never arrived at a state of casual undress around each other, even on the mornings after their lovemaking.

If only he hadn't left me those nights, she groaned now to herself, we might have had a chance. Now it was too late. She had slept badly herself, torn between the thought that she had been a fool to give up hope and the conviction that she simply was incapable of going on the way they had been.

'It's all right,' she said in a muffled voice. 'It was partially my fault. I handled the whole thing badly.'

She knew he was watching her, but she still couldn't face him. After a long pause, he went on in a stiff, formal tone.

'I still don't pretend to understand what's behind this sudden decision of yours, but I do recall clearly assuring you from the beginning that you could back out at any time. I want you to know I intend to honour that promise.'

Finally, she looked up at him, and her heart choked in her throat at the weary look on his face. 'What do you want to do?' she asked.

He shrugged. 'Nothing. Go on as we were before. . .' His voice trailed off, and he turned to go. 'I'll be late tonight,' he said in a brisker tone as he walked towards the front door. 'Martin said last night that everyone in Washington is anxious for a report on the Palestine trip. Don't wait dinner for me.'

When he was gone, Paula sat for a long time at the breakfast table, crumbling her toast and drinking cup after cup of bitter coffee. She knew there was no use going over and over the same ground. She had made her decision, done the only thing she could.

It will be all right, she thought, as she walked slowly into her room to get started on her latest commission. It will have to be.

Summer began to fade into autumn, and by the end of September, the leaves on the giant oaks and maples along the Potomac and on the capitol grounds were turning, spreading a canopy of gold over the city streets and parks. There was an autumn nip in the air now, and the morning fogs began to roll in, damp and chill.

Paula and Matthew had managed to resume their old life, after a fashion. It would never really be the same again, she thought from time to time, but it was a tolerable existence, better, certainly, than the walking death her life had been after Richard died and before she met Matthew.

After their last talk that morning a month ago, the subject had never been mentioned again. True to his word, Matthew not only stayed out of her bedroom, but had given up showing her any of the small signs of affection she had come to enjoy. He never touched her at all, now, unless it was unavoidable, and then only politely, as a gesture of courtesy.

She missed this dreadfully, and it crossed her mind many times that she'd been a fool to throw away the little bit of affection and passion Matthew was able to give her. She found herself often on the verge of telling him she'd changed her mind again and wanted him, wanted his child, on any terms.

Then, without planning it, she would pass by his bedroom again, as if drawn there by an invisible magnet, and see the photograph of Beth still there on his bedside table in its place of honour, and she strengthened her resolve to keep Matthew out of her heart.

This was difficult to do. Even though they lived like virtual strangers, whenever they were together she would find herself staring at him at a crowded social gathering, watching his mouth as he smiled or spoke to someone, the graceful way he moved across a room or held a drink, hearing his deep voice raised in laughter at a joke.

She tried also to steel herself against the tormenting pangs of jealousy that assailed her when she saw him dancing or talking with other women. She couldn't bear to see the way his eyes lit up and the firm mouth softened when a beautiful woman put a hand on his arm as she spoke to him, or around his neck while dancing with him.

By now the fall social season in Washington was in full swing, with Margaret, of course, in the vanguard. One of her first forays into action was to hold a dinner dance at the Mayflower Hotel in honour of a freshman senator from California. She had rented one of the smaller dining rooms for the occasion, and had kept her plans for decoration a mysterious secret.

Of course, she insisted that Matthew and Paula attend, and on that Saturday night they dutifully presented themselves at the appointed hour. They stepped into a room decorated in a modified disco fashion. The pop band was blaring in the already crowded room, and a brilliant strobe lamp flashed swiftly changing colours over the dancers and the band.

'How do you like it?' Margaret cried when she greeted them.

'It's—overwhelming,' Paula said dubiously, glancing around in dismay. The music was deafening.

'Isn't it wonderful?' Margaret was clearly pleased with the sensation she was causing. She leaned closer and lowered her voice. 'It's only for immediate effect. Shock value. I've arranged with the band to tone it down to our usual speed as soon as everyone loosens up.'

She had arranged the tables so that a small circular area next to the bandstand was cleared for dancing, and a few hardy couples were out there now attempting the modern dance steps to the pounding beat of the rock music.

There were brightly coloured placemats on the tables and little flickering lamps in odd plastic shapes. A buffet was set up at the far end of the room next to the bar, where champagne, martinis and scotch were dispensed freely by a bored-looking bartender in a white coat.

As they followed Margaret to their table, Paula saw several familiar faces. Everyone seemed to be having a good time, she thought, as she smiled and waved at the people she knew. Michele Lathrop was there with the senator from California in tow. Beryl Armitage and her husband were at a table with the Pittingers, and David Wyatt was on the dance floor doing a creditable frug with a young Congresswoman from Georgia.

'Just do your own thing,' Margaret said as she pointed out their table. 'This is a *loose* party. Eat when you're hungry, drink when you're thirsty, and dance when the spirit moves you.'

With that she fluttered off into the crowd to greet the latest arrivals.

William was sitting stiffly at the table, red-faced and uncomfortable. 'Well,' he said miserably as they joined him, 'what do you think of your sister's latest escapade?'

Poor William, Paula thought. He had a lot to contend with. 'It's interesting,' she hedged, glancing around at the crowd.

'I think you can trust Margaret,' Matthew said unexpectedly. 'She knows what she's doing.'

William sighed and shook his head. 'I don't know. It's those boys of ours. Told us we were so far behind the times we were growing mould. Margaret takes as gospel every word they utter. Says we've got to keep up with the times.'

Taking her cue from Matthew, Paula put a hand on William's arm and said, 'You just wait, William. Soon every society hostess in the city will be putting on disco parties. Margaret is a pacesetter, not a follower. You know that.'

William brightened. 'Do you really think so?' Happily, he rose and followed Matthew to the bar for drinks.

While they were gone, Margaret came back to the table with Michele and Senator Larkin, the guest of honour. She introduced the senator to Paula, and when William and Matthew returned with a bottle of champagne and six glasses, they all sat down and tried to carry on a conversation over the blaring music.

Paula gave up after a few abortive attempts and leaned back in her chair, sipping champagne and watching the others. Michele was sitting across the table between Matthew and Senator Larkin, a tall blond god who looked as though he had spent his whole life up to now surfing on the California beaches.

Michele appeared ecstatic, glorying in the attentions of the two handsome men, who leaned across her from time to time in order to speak to each other over the din of the music. She was wearing an extremely low-cut white dress, no more than a slinky slip, brilliant against her heavy tan and long mane of golden hair.

True to Margaret's word, in about an hour, the rock band toned down to a more moderate beat and a softer level of sound. The strobe light went out, and the party began to take on the more familiar subdued tenor of Washington parties.

Senator Larkin asked Margaret to dance, and before Paula could catch Matthew's eye, she saw Michele leap to her feet and put out a hand to him. Why doesn't she stick to her own man? Paula wondered irritably, and why did Matthew have that fatuous grin on his face? Really, the woman was a menace.

She watched as he pushed back his chair and took Michele's hand in his. He stood up, and the hand moved around her waist. He was smiling down at her, and as she turned into his arms on the dance floor, Paula saw both her hands move up to rest on Matthew's shoulders, the red-tipped fingers sliding possessively over the fabric of his dark suit.

That's my husband she's manhandling, Paula thought in a sudden spurt of irritation. As she watched them slowly dance their way into the crowd on the floor, she had a sudden recollection of the first night she had met Matthew. He had danced with Michele, then, too, and Paula remembered now what a handsome couple she thought they made.

She danced with William, who seemed much happier now that the party had settled down along more conservative lines.

'You and Matthew were right, Paula,' he said as he guided her sedately around the floor.

Paula turned her attention to him with an effort. She had just caught a glimpse of Matthew and Michele dancing by, cheek to cheek, their bodies plastered together. Michele was whispering in his ear, and Matthew appeared to be delighted at whatever it was she was saying.

'What?' Paula asked William. 'Right about what?'

'The party, of course.' He waved a hand. 'She got everyone loosened up, and now they're all having a marvellous time.'

'Yes,' Paula agreed in a wry tone. 'They're loosened up, all right.' And my husband among them, she added to herself.

As the evening progressed, Paula could hardly keep her eyes off Michele and Matthew. Even when they weren't dancing, Michele monopolised his attention at the table, leaning seductively towards him as they conversed in low tones, putting a hand on his arm, fingering the lapel of his black jacket.

He seems to be enjoying it, Paula thought, watching the black head bend close to Michele's, laughing at her jokes, actually flirting with her. Really, Paula thought crossly, that dress is too much! Or, rather, too little! The white silk clung sensuously to every curve, and when she leaned over, the deep vee neckline revealed a good portion of the full breasts.

Paula felt positively dowdy in her old black dress with the beaded white jacket, almost three years old, now. At least it fit her better now than it had last winter, but she decided that she'd have to start paying more attention to her clothes.

Matthew asked her to dance at last, after two dances with the clinging Michele and one with Margaret. By now, Paula was really angry. She wasn't jealous, she told herself, she just hated to see her husband make a fool of himself.

Sitting at the table, seething, she had drunk glass after glass of champagne, and when she stood up now to dance with Matthew, her head spun ominously. She put down her glass. No more of that, she promised herself.

She looked at Matthew, waiting for her patiently by her chair, a half-smile on the handsome face, a gleam of pleasure in the grey eyes, put there, no doubt, Paula thought bitterly, by the attentions of the beautiful Michele. Then a wicked thought suddenly came to her.

He's *my* husband, damn it, she said to herself. If anyone is going to put that light in his eyes, it'll be me! Casually, without looking at him, she slipped off the beaded jacket and laid it on the back of her chair.

When she went into his arms, he held her loosely at a distance, as was his custom, and began to move out on to the dance floor. No, she said to herself recklessly, not this time. Not tonight. She moved closer to him, slid her arms up to his shoulders, then clasped her hands behind his neck.

He simply stopped short, right on the dance floor, and looked down at her, a puzzled frown on his face. She fluttered her thick eyelashes and gazed up at him demurely.

'What's wrong, Matthew?' she asked, giving him what she hoped was a seductive smile. She began to twine her fingers through the black hair above the nape of his neck and pressed herself up against him.

She felt him draw in a breath, saw the grey eyes widen momentarily, then his arms came around her, holding her closer. The strong thighs pressed against hers, and he started dancing again.

'Nothing's wrong,' he murmured, his breath warm in her ear. 'Nothing at all.'

As they danced in the dim smoky room, their arms around each other, their faces pressed together, Paula's anger gradually faded, and a slow, languorous warmth began to steal through her. She was still a little dizzy from the champagne she had drunk, but she knew the exquisite sensations rippling through her body had nothing to do with wine.

Matthew had placed one of his hands flat against her bare back, over the low bodice of the black dress. It was moving slowly now, warm and strong, and she felt his lips on her cheek. She closed her eyes, swaying a little in his arms.

Then his mouth was at her ear, his breath soft and sensuous. 'Let's get out of here,' he murmured. 'Let's go home.'

She drew her head back a little and opened her eyes. She looked up at Matthew, and the silvery eyes glowed down at her. The finely carved mouth was relaxed, the lines of tension on his face smoothed out. He's so handsome, she thought, so tall, so strong. She felt giddy with desire and love.

She ran her hand up over the back of his neck and into his hair. 'Yes,' she whispered. 'Yes.'

Still in a daze, Paula allowed him to lead her off the floor, but by the time he had retrieved her jacket and coat and they'd said their goodbyes to the rest of the party, she was beginning to have second thoughts about the explosive situation she'd manoeuvred herself into.

Outside in the cool evening air, as they walked towards the car, her head cleared considerably, and she realised with dismay that in her fit of pique over Michele's possessive attitude, she had initiated something she knew she couldn't go through with.

As they strode along the sidewalk, Matthew's arm was clamped tightly around her shoulder, holding her closely against him. When they reached the car, she glanced up at him out of the corner of her eye, shivering a little at the look of intense concentration on the strong face.

He glanced down at her. 'Cold?' he asked, pulling her closer.

She smiled weakly. 'A little.'

He kissed her briefly, then opened the door of

the Mercedes and handed her inside. What in the world am I going to do? she thought as she waited for him to get in. How am I going to get out of this?

They didn't speak at all during the short drive home or in the elevator going up to the apartment. Paula tried to think, but nothing came to her. All her fine resolutions had gone out the window. She cursed Michele Lathrop, but in her heart she knew it was her own petty jealousy that had landed her in this awful position.

Inside the apartment, Matthew flicked the switch that turned on the dim lamp by the sofa, shut the door to the hall behind him and put his keys in his jacket pocket. She had turned her back to him and was starting to shrug out of her coat, wondering if she shouldn't just say a casual goodnight and go off to her own bedroom without any lengthy explanations. She dreaded a scene.

Then, before she could decide, she felt him pulling the coat off her shoulders and down her arms. His head came down, his mouth in her hair, and he tossed the coat on to a nearby chair. She stood there, paralysed, as his arms came around her, and glanced down to see them around her waist, firm and possessive.

His mouth was at her ear now, murmuring softly, 'I want you, Paula. God, how I want you.'

Her heart leapt at his words, and when he started tugging at the short beaded jacket, a mindless lassitude stole over her. She felt him leave her momentarily as he shrugged out of his own jacket and tossed them both on to the chair with her coat.

In that moment, she knew she had to stop him before it was too late and her own desire betrayed her. If she let this go on, gave in to her feelings, there would only be more heartache ahead for her when he retreated again to worship at Beth's shrine. She couldn't bear that. Not again.

When his hands came back to settle on her bare shoulders, she took a step away from him and whirled around to face him. He had taken off his tie and unbuttoned his shirt. She stared for a moment at the long column of his throat, the glimpse of bare tanned chest, the brilliant grey eyes, then steeled herself.

In a clear firm voice, she announced, 'Matthew, I'm going to bed now. Alone.'

It was the only way she could do it, but when she saw the look of blank incomprehension on his face, she immediately regretted her brutal tone. Then the grey eyes flashed with sudden anger. Her heart started to beat rapidly, and she struggled to remain calm and composed. Naturally, he would resent what she had done, she told herself, but Matthew was a gentleman. He had complete control over his emotions. She had nothing to fear from him.

'No,' he said thickly at last. 'You can't do that.'

She lifted her chin. 'I'm sorry. I have to. Surely you understand. . .'

'Understand!' he growled, taking the step towards her that separated them and grasping her roughly around the neck. 'That's all I've been doing for the past month!'

His face was flushed with fury and the large strong hand at the back of her head was pulling her hair, hurting her.

'Matthew,' she said weakly, 'I know how you must feel. . .'

'No, damn it,' he shouted, 'you don't know how I feel! It's one thing for you to banish me from your bed when you keep a decent distance between us. That's difficult enough, living here in the same apartment with you. But when you deliberately tease me, lead me on, and then back off, that's something else again.'

Paula's eyes widened in fear at the harsh tone, and she stared up at the menacing dark face looming over her. This wasn't the Matthew she knew. This was a stranger, threatening, dangerous, out of control.

'I didn't mean . . .' she faltered.

An ugly sneer twisted on his mouth. 'You didn't mean! You don't know what you mean, do you, Paula? One night you melt in my arms, the next you're a block of ice. Well, I've had enough! You're going to finish what you started out on that dance floor, or I'm going to take it by force.'

Both hands were around her neck now, almost choking her, and she was badly frightened. What would he do? Rape her? Kill her?

His mouth came down on hers, hard and grinding, drawing blood as her teeth bit into her soft inner lips. She struggled, moaning, as his tongue forced her lips apart and invaded her mouth, but the more she fought him, the more firmly he held her.

He tore his mouth away and drew back, glaring down at her, his eyes wild, his face suffused with naked desire. She cowered back from him, the green eyes pleading, but her fear only seemed to inflame him further.

He reached out a hand and clutched the low bodice of her dress. In one abrupt, powerful movement he yanked it down so that the centre seam ripped apart and the black material fell away, leaving her bare breasts half-exposed.

'Matthew,' she whispered. 'Don't. Don't do this.'

'You asked for it,' he ground out, the grey eyes flashing, 'and you're going to get it.'

She stood rigid and trembling while he pulled the ruined dress roughly off her shoulders until it dropped on the floor at her feet. He was like a maniac, pulling now at her underpants until they too were ripped away. She didn't even recognise him. His hands came back to her bare body and began kneading her breasts painfully. She could hear his rasping breath, feel its harshness on her mouth as he claimed it once again.

Then he swooped her up roughly into his arms and carried her down the hall to her bedroom. After he dropped her carelessly on the bed, he stood up, glaring down at her naked form. She lay there, frozen with fear, watching him in the dim light from the hall as he took off his shirt, then unbuckled his belt and slipped out of the dark trousers.

Should she try to get away? How could she? Where could she run to, naked, in the middle of the night? She couldn't fight him. She was no match for his superior strength, especially in his aroused state. The best thing she could do was lie there and let him use her body until his passion and fury were spent.

He was on the bed kneeling over her now, the palms of his hands firmly planted on either side of her head, his broad shoulders and powerful bare chest heaving. She looked up at the dark head poised over her, the eyes glazed with lustful anger, the dishevelled hair falling over his forehead.

She bit her lip and turned her head away on the pillow, choking back a sob. 'Please, Matthew,' she groaned. 'Not like this.'

For a moment, she felt him pause and stiffen. Then he lowered himself on top of her and she heard him speak as if from a great distance. 'It's too late, Paula. I've got to finish what you started.'

His mouth was at her breast now, pulling greedily at the peak while his hand moved over her other breast. To her horror, she felt her nipples harden under his lips and hand, and she began to move beneath him, responding to him against her will, matching his fierce desire as a liquid fire coursed through her bloodstream.

When he took her at last, she cried out, clutching at him, with him all the way, until they reached the peak together. Then, passion spent at last, he slumped down against her and they fell apart, exhausted.

With a groan he rolled away from her to the other side of the bed. Paula lay there beside him, her whole body sore from his violent lovemaking. She could hear his laboured breathing and longed for him to take her in his arms, to comfort her, tell her he loved her. The short distance between them in the bed could have been a million miles.

She glanced over at him out of the corner of her eye. He was quieter now, lying on his back with one arm thrown over his forehead, his eyes closed. A wave of despair passed over her at his cold rejection, and the tears began to gather, spilling slowly down her cheeks.

Suddenly, she felt his weight shift and heard him get out of the bed. Without a word or a glance, he bent down to pick up his clothes and walked slowly out of the room.

After he had gone, Paula lay sobbing silently in the darkness. This was worse, she thought, far worse than when she had lost Richard. That had been a clean pain, searing in its intensity, but ultimately purifying and strengthening her.

This hopeless love she felt for Matthew was degrading. It pulled her down, weakened her. Not only was her response to him more violent than it had been to Richard's gentler lovemaking, but there was no future for her in it. He didn't love her. He never would. And tonight proved to her that she couldn't continue to live with him under the old arrangement. It wasn't possible. She'd have to leave.

The next morning Paula woke up with every bone and muscle in her body aching. She stumbled into the bathroom, and when she stood under the shower, she could see bruises on her burning skin.

It was late. Matthew was gone. He had made coffee, and Paula warmed it up, then sat drinking it at the kitchen table thinking over what she should do, where she should go.

She hated to go running to Margaret, but there was really no other alternative. It would be better to have to put up with her sister's probing questions and unwanted advice than to be alone right now.

After what happened last night, she felt tattered. Her nerves were in shreds. She had to get away, try to mend the ragged edges of herself, her life, together again. She felt so tired, she thought, as she dragged herself to the telephone at last.

When she heard Margaret's bright, confident voice on the line, she had to resist the impulse to slam the receiver down. How could she face her? Yet, did she have a choice?

'Margaret, it's me. Paula. Would it be all right if I came out to stay with you for a while?'

There was a short silence. Then, cautiously, Margaret said, 'Well, of course. You know I'd love to have you any time. Is Matthew going off on another trip so soon?'

What could she say? She couldn't lie and say yes, but on the other hand, she didn't need to volunteer anything. Margaret would ferret out the truth soon enough, but for now Paula just couldn't stand talking about it.

'I'll tell you about it when I get there,' she finally said. 'Would it be all right if I come today? Before noon?' She wanted to leave as soon as she'd packed. She couldn't bear to face Matthew. She'd leave him a note.

'Of course,' Margaret said. 'Come any time you like. I have a hair appointment at eleven. If I'm not here, you know where the key is.'

After she had hung up Paula went into her room to pack. She wouldn't need much right away, and could always come back later, when she was calmer, to get the rest of her things.

When she had finished packing the bare essentials and stacked the drawings for the job she was working on in a large cardboard portfolio, she put on a rust-coloured corduroy trouser suit and stood at her dressing-table mirror brushing her hair.

Gazing at her reflection, she was surprised to see how normal she looked. Aside from faint smudges under the green eyes, they sparkled brightly. Her short black hair, freshly washed that morning, shone as she brushed it. How misleading appearances can be, she thought, when she was breaking inside.

When she was through, she slung her handbag over her shoulder and picked up the suitcase and portfolio, ready to leave. She glanced around the familiar room at the neatly made bed, the bare dressing table, the work table in the corner by the window. A shaft of golden autumn sunshine streamed in on to the patterned rug. The room looked serene and tidy. She'd miss it.

She turned to go, then, and as she started down the hallway, she heard a familiar noise at the front door. Matthew, she thought, listening to the turn of the key in the lock, the door opening and closing. Her heart simply stopped, and she stood there, paralysed, unable to move, a sickening wave of dizziness passing over her.

Then she heard his footsteps coming towards her. Her heart gave one great lurch, then started to pound in a dull, heavy thud. She glanced up. He was standing not ten feet from her at the end of the hall, staring at her with a blank expression.

For one moment, Paula had second thoughts about leaving him. He looked very tall, very handsome, very self-possessed. Yet even at this distance, she could see the lines of pain on his face.

I've made him unhappy, too, she thought. I put those marks of suffering there. All she wanted in that split second was to run to him, throw herself into his arms and tell him how much she loved him.

Then the moment passed. 'I—I didn't expect you to come home,' she stammered at last.

'No,' he said quietly. His eyes flicked to the suitcase in her hand, the portfolio under her arm. 'You're leaving.'

'Yes, I am.' Her voice sounded shaky in her ears. 'I must get away.'

He only stared, obviously mulling this over in his mind. Then, 'Where will you be?' he asked finally.

'At Margaret's. But please don't. . .'

He frowned and held up a hand. 'Don't worry. I won't come after you.' He took a step towards her, one hand outstretched, then sighed deeply and let the hand fall to his side. 'I came home this morning to apologise for last night.'

'Please,' she broke in breathlessly. 'There's no need. It was my own fault. I asked for it.'

He shook his head, the frown deepening. 'Even so, that's no excuse for—for *attacking* you the way I did.'

'Perhaps not,' she said in a brisker tone, 'but the fact remains that I did provoke you into it. Deliberately,' she added with a lift to her chin. This was no time to hedge or play games.

He gave her a puzzled look. 'Why?' he asked softly.

She shrugged. 'I can't explain. I don't really understand it myself.' She gave him a long look. 'That's one of the things I need to sort out, one of the reasons I've got to leave.'

He bent his dark head, deep in thought for a moment, then nodded. 'Yes. I can see that.'

He looked so miserable, she thought with a sudden rush of sympathy. Why? Surely he's as anxious to get rid of me as I am to go. She recalled the hatred in his eyes last night, the violence in him when he ripped her dress off her, threw her on the bed.

Then a thought occurred to her. 'I won't do anything, well, *legal*,' she said in a rush, 'if you don't want me to. I don't want to cause a scandal or harm your career.'

His mouth quirked in a bitter smile. 'Were you thinking of having me arrested for raping my wife?' he asked quietly. 'I understand that's done in some States now.'

She flushed deeply and bit her lip. 'Of course not. It wasn't rape and you know it.' Their eyes met briefly. 'I was talking about a divorce.'

'Oh, that,' he said. 'Do what you please about that. My career won't suffer. People forget.'

'Very well,' she said stiffly. 'I'd better go. I told Margaret I'd be out some time before noon.'

She started down the hall towards him, her step brisk and purposeful. She only wanted to get out of there, away from his disturbing presence. When she reached him, he stepped aside to let her pass.

'Goodbye then, Paula,' he said softly.

She couldn't look at him. 'Goodbye, Matthew.'

Her eyes were stinging with unshed tears, and it wasn't until she had gone down the elevator to the basement garage, stowed her gear in the boot of the red Corvette and got inside that she let go. She laid her forehead down on the steering wheel and sobbed.

CHAPTER NINE

'I should think you would have learned by now, Paula,' Margaret was saying in an exasperated tone, 'that it only does harm to hold it all in. Now, for the last time, will you please tell me what's going on?'

Paula laid down her pencil with a sigh and looked up at her sister. They were in the small attic room at Margaret's that Paula used as a studio, and she was hard at work trying to get some holiday drawings finished for the Philadelphia store before Thanksgiving.

'All right,' she said at last. 'What do you want to know?'

Margaret plumped herself down on the rickety wooden chair beside Paula's work table with a grunt of satisfaction.

'I really don't mean to pry,' she said in a kinder tone. 'I understand that it's your nature to keep your troubles to yourself, but I just need to know what's going on between you and Matthew. You've been here for over a month now, and every time I even mention his name, you either bite my head off or disappear.'

Paula gazed out the window at the bleak November landscape. The leaves were all gone from the trees and soon it would be winter again. Another cold, icy winter alone. She turned to her sister.

'There's really nothing to tell. We've agreed on a temporary separation, that's all.'

'But why?' Margaret wailed. 'You seemed so happy together, just right for each other.' She gave Paula a sharp look. 'Something must have happened. Was it another woman?' When Paula's eyes flew open in alarm at the suggestion, Margaret smiled grimly. 'I see I've hit a nerve. Was he unfaithful? I can't believe that of Matthew. He's not the type.'

Paula looked down at her hands, idly toying with the pencil. 'No,' she said slowly. 'It wasn't another woman.' She paused. In a sense this wasn't true. There *was* another woman—Beth— although not the way Margaret meant it.

'Well, then?' Margaret prompted.

Paula took a deep breath. 'Matthew is still in love with his first wife. Beth.'

For a long moment, Margaret only stared at her. Then, briskly, she said, 'That's nonsense! Anyone could see he was crazy about you. He treated you as though you were made of glass, and I caught him several times looking at you as though he'd like to eat you. No,' she shook her head vigorously, 'Matthew loves you.'

Paula smiled stiffly. It did no good to try to explain to Margaret. 'You're wrong,' she said at last. 'Oh, I think Matthew likes me and wants me, but he never loved me. Not the way he loved Beth.'

The two sisters sat in silence for some time. Paula hated having to discuss her marriage with anyone. She had had no contact with Matthew at all in the six weeks she'd been at Margaret's, but hardly a day, an hour, a minute passed that she didn't think of him and miss him.

Several times she had been tempted to call him, just to hear his voice, but she knew that would only make it harder for her in the long run. She had to make a clean break.

'What are you going to do?' Margaret asked finally.

Paula shrugged. 'I don't know. We haven't really discussed it. Get a divorce, I suppose, eventually.'

Margaret gave a small snort of impatience. 'I think you're out of your mind. What do you care if he thinks he still loves this Beth? She's gone. You're alive. I *know* Matthew loves you in his way. Can't you just accept what he's able to give and make a life together?'

Paula gave her sister a long, bleak look. 'I could,' she replied quietly, 'except that I'm hopelessly in love with him.'

Margaret only stared. 'I see,' she said slowly at last. Paula cringed under the pitying look.

Then Margaret jumped to her feet. 'Well, I must get busy. It's almost noon and I haven't begun to get things ready for the party. Hilda is making. . .'

'Party!' Paula exclaimed. 'What party?'

Margaret put her hands on her hips and gave her sister a disgusted look. 'The party I've been planning for the past three weeks, of course. Don't tell me you've forgotten.'

'No,' Paula said slowly. 'I hadn't forgotten. I just didn't think it would be so soon.' She raised her eyes in sudden suspicion. 'Have you invited Matthew?'

Margaret reddened and patted her hair nervously. 'Well, yes, to be honest, I did.'

'Well, then, I won't go,' Paula stated flatly.

'He declined,' Margaret rushed ahead. 'He said he'd be out of town.' She paused. 'He asked about you when I called him.'

'What did you tell him?'

Margaret shrugged. 'Just that I didn't understand you and never had. He seemed concerned about you.' She waited, but when Paula didn't answer, she gave another exasperated exclamation, then turned and stalked out of the room.

Paula turned back to her work, relieved the painful discussion was finally over. She hated talking about it. Of course, he would be concerned. That didn't mean he wanted her back. One word, she thought, one movement towards her, and she knew she would have gone back to him on any terms.

She stared down at the half-finished drawing on the table before her. Why hadn't he called her? But then, she had left him, she reasoned. Maybe he was waiting for her to call him. Could they ever get back on the old footing again?

There was something else. She had begun to suspect that she might possibly be pregnant. As yet, it was only a faint possibility, too soon to tell. If it was true, they might be able to resume their original 'arrangement' and make it work, with a child to consider.

Then she thought of that last night they'd spent together, the hatred in the grey eyes, the unleashed violence of his lovemaking, brutal, punishing, unyielding. She shivered a little and picked up her pencil again. No one had ever treated her like that before in her life, she thought, trying to concentrate on her work. Certainly Richard hadn't.

But no one, not even her dead husband, had ever aroused her to the pitch of passion Matthew had, either.

There was no way Paula could get out of putting

in at least a token appearance at Margaret's party. Fifty people had been invited, and although the house was large, they'd be all over the place. She couldn't just hide in her room.

She waited to make her appearance downstairs until well after all the guests had arrived and the noise of the party drifted up to her bedroom. Most of her clothes were still at the apartment in town, and all she had to wear was the black dress she had on that last night she'd spent there. While at Margaret's, she had carefully mended the ripped front seam where Matthew had torn it in his fury.

When she slipped unobtrusively into the dining room where the bar had been set up, she was relieved to see that William was standing there talking to David Wyatt and two other men on the President's staff. William looked so comfortable, she thought, so solid and reassuring, and she saw his eyes light up as she walked slowly towards him.

'Paula,' he greeted her warmly, putting an arm around her shoulders. 'Here you are. Will you have a drink?'

'Yes, please,' she murmured. 'Hello, David,' she said, turning to the stocky blond man. 'I haven't seen you for quite a while. How have you been?'

'Oh, same as usual,' he replied, flashing her his famous boyish grin. 'Trying to stay out of trouble.'

She laughed. 'Do you find that so difficult? What have you been up to?'

William handed her a drink and she took a grateful swallow. It wasn't so bad, she thought. These people are all my friends.

David had launched into a long explanation of the latest battle in the House, something to do with a trade-off between a Congressman from Alabama and one from Kansas that involved peanut farmers and cattle ranchers. She couldn't quite follow it, but David made it sound so humorous as he imitated the two parties, that soon she was laughing along with the others.

Paula hadn't felt so lighthearted in months. She had been wrong, she decided now, to bury herself in her work, hiding out at her sister's house in Virginia. It was time to start living again. Even without Matthew, if necessary.

Then she saw him, and the laughter died on her lips. He had suddenly just appeared in the doorway, tall and striking-looking in his dark suit, the grey eyes fixed firmly upon her in a long, hard stare. Almost choking on her drink and swaying a little at the impact his presence had on her, she instinctively reached out a hand to grasp William's arm for support. Had Margaret lied to her when she said he wasn't coming tonight?

He was walking slowly towards them now. The others hadn't noticed anything, she was grateful to see. David still had the floor, and their attention was firmly fixed on him.

Paula knew there was no hope of avoiding Matthew now, and when he came to stand by her side, a little apart from the others, she released William's arm and moved back a step. Then, her heart still pounding wildly, she looked up at him.

'Hello, Matthew,' she said in a low shaky voice.

'Paula,' he said shortly with a curt nod. 'How are you?'

'I'm fine,' she said, forcing a weak smile.

'I can see that,' he went on bitterly. 'You seem to be having a good time.' He glanced at David, who was just winding up his story, his appreciative audience roaring helplessly by now. He looked down at her gravely. 'I'd like to talk to you.'

She thought a moment. They'd have to talk eventually. It might as well be now. 'Come into the study,' she said. 'I don't think we'll be disturbed.'

During this brief exchange they had gradually started moving away from the others. They continued on now out of the room and down the long carpeted hall to William's study. When they were inside, Paula shut the door behind them and stood watching him, waiting to see what he would say.

A small fire was burning in the grate, and a lamp shone dimly on William's large oak desk, set squarely in the middle of the room. The walls were lined with books, and a large globe stood in the corner by a window. It was not a large room, and with the fire and the soft light, it seemed uncomfortably intimate to Paula now that the noise of the party had been shut out.

Matthew stood with his back to the fire, facing her, his legs slightly apart, his hands clasped behind him, a frown on the fine features.

'I won't beat about the bush, Paula,' he said at last. 'I came tonight to ask you to come back. I had it all planned. I knew you didn't want to see me—you hadn't contacted me once in all these weeks—so I told Margaret I wasn't coming.' His mouth twisted in a parody of a smile. 'I was going to take you by surprise, sweep you off your feet. Then when I walked in and saw you with Wyatt, the way you looked at him, laughed with him, I could see it was hopeless. All *I* ever seemed able to do was make you cry,' he ended on a note of regret.

'That's not true!' she cried. 'David Wyatt means nothing to me. He never did. He's merely entertaining. I never wanted you to entertain me.'

'What did you want, Paula?' he shot back.

She longed to say that all she ever wanted was for him to love her, but the words stuck in her throat. She couldn't answer. He crossed over to where she stood by William's desk and looked down at her.

'I miss you, Paula,' he said bleakly. 'Will you come back? Will you try again? I promise I won't touch you, won't come near you.'

She bit her lip and glanced away, her mind racing. She was sorely tempted. It was what she wanted, wasn't it? But could they make it on those terms? Could they go back to their old platonic relationship after what had passed between them? She thought of her suspicion that she might be pregnant. That would make all the difference. If she was, indeed, carrying Matthew's child, she should go back to him.

She looked up at him. 'Let me think about it, Matthew. Give me a week or two.'

He nodded. 'Yes, of course.' A little light appeared then in the silvery eyes, warming Paula as she gazed into them. He may not love me, she thought, but I know now he really does want me to be his wife.

He left, then, and she didn't see him the rest of the evening. Apparently, he had gone home.

Paula drove into town the following week to see Dr Banks. She had called on Monday, insisting that she had to see him as soon as possible, and his accommodating nurse had managed to squeeze her in for an appointment on Wednesday.

After the examination was over, she sat in his office clutching her handbag, anxiously awaiting his diagnosis.

'Well, my dear, I'd say you show all the signs of

an expectant mother,' he said at last, beaming. 'I'll do another test, to be positive, but there's really no doubt in my mind.'

Paula thanked him and drove back to Virginia in a daze. Matthew's child, she thought over and over again. I'm carrying Matthew's child. She knew now she would go back to him. They could have a good life together. The torment of living without him was far worse than the torment of living with him without love. At least this way, she could hope.

'Well, I'm glad of that,' Margaret said in a positive tone when Paula announced her decision to go back to Matthew that afternoon. 'You're choosing the wisest course. You'd be a fool to let a man like Matthew Stratton get away from you.'

Paula only smiled. Margaret didn't begin to understand the true nature of her relationship with Matthew, and she had no intention of enlightening her. She hadn't told her about the baby, either. Matthew had the right to hear the news first.

Ever since her visit to Dr Banks that morning and the subsequent decision to go back to Matthew, Paula had felt a deep sense of calm at last, a sense of rightness. She knew there were hurdles ahead, but with a baby coming, it was worth fighting to save her marriage.

'When will you leave?' Margaret asked now.

They were sitting in front of the living-room fire drinking tea. It was raining out, another cold, bleak November day. Only this winter, Paula thought, leaning back in her chair and closing her eyes, I won't be alone.

'Tomorrow,' she replied at last. She opened her eyes and exchanged a smile with her sister. 'I came with so little that I have hardly any packing to do.'

'I'm so glad, Paula,' Margaret said in a low unsteady voice. She brushed her eyes lightly with her fingertips. 'All I ever wanted was for you to be happy.'

'Oh, stop it, you idiot,' Paula teased. The sight of her sister's happy tears moved her deeply. 'There are no guarantees it will work. You might have me on your hands again.'

'Oh, no,' Margaret said fervently. 'If you leave that man again, *I* won't take you in.'

CHAPTER TEN

THE apartment seemed very quiet when Paula let herself in late the next afternoon. She went straight to her room and unpacked her things, hanging the few clothes she had taken with her back in the wardrobe, setting out her toilet articles on the bare dressing table, and putting away her underwear in the chest of drawers.

She went into the kitchen to make herself a cup of tea. There was hardly a trace of Matthew there. A glass and a cup had been rinsed and were turned upside down on the counter to drain, but other than that the room looked as though no one had entered it since she left. He had probably eaten his meals out, she thought.

Then an idea came to her. Why not cook him a nice dinner? It would be a good way of letting him know she was home to stay. She glanced through the cupboards and refrigerator. There wasn't much to work with, she soon saw. A half dozen eggs, a quart of milk, an unopened pound of butter, some canned soup.

There was a boneless cooked ham in the freezer. She could make an omelette. Tomorrow she would go shopping, stock up the nearly empty shelves and barren fridge. Matthew needed taking care of, she thought, a fierce rush of love filling her heart. He needs me.

She set the ham out on the kitchen counter to thaw and with her mug of tea in her hand, she wandered through the apartment. It was good to see her own things again in the living room, the rust-coloured sofa, the small gold chairs. I'll build a fire later, she thought, give him a cheerful cosy place to come home to.

It was a beautiful apartment, with limitless possibilities once she set her mind to it and gave up her former tentative feeling about her marriage. They could start entertaining more at home. Matthew would like that.

She continued her inspection, her mind occupied with plans for the future, until she found herself just outside Matthew's bedroom. She stopped short. The door was open.

On an impulse, she stepped inside, her eyes darting immediately, instinctively, to the bedside table where she had seen Beth's silver-framed photograph. It was gone! Paula caught her breath sharply. What did it mean? A wild hope surged within her. Then, sobering, she thought, perhaps he's out of town and had taken it with him.

Of course, she decided, her spirits drooping. The cold apartment, the barren cupboards, the spotless kitchen. He was gone. She should have called him first before she came. She glanced at her watch. It was six o'clock. Ordinarily he would have been home by now.

She went back into the kitchen and rinsed out her cup. Nothing has changed, she thought dully. A wave of despair passed over her. It was dark outside now, she could see through the kitchen window, and the rain spat against the blackened pane, driven by a sudden gust of wind. She glanced around the spotless kitchen sadly. It was hard now to recall her happy plans of just a few minutes ago.

Then she noticed a newspaper lying folded up in a far corner of the counter. Idly, she unfolded it and glanced down at the date. November the twentieth. That was today. He must have been here this morning, at any rate. She frowned. There was a significance to that date. What was it? She stood there, pondering, for several moments, and then it dawned on her.

November the twentieth was the anniversary of Beth's death! How could she have forgotten? What a stupid day to pick to come back! Wherever Matthew was he was most likely off on his annual drunk, the photograph of his dead wife with him, his thoughts immersed in her.

She stood there shivering uncontrollably. The apartment seemed so cold all of a sudden. Her first impulse was to run, to leave, to come back another day, perhaps not to come back at all. Then she thought of the child she was carrying, her resolution to make a life with Matthew no matter what it cost.

Was she going to run away at the first disappointment? I won't give up, she thought. She squared her shoulders with renewed determination and strode purposefully into the hall and turned up the heat. I'll have a little supper, she decided, shower and make a fire. Even if I have to spend the evening all by myself, it'll make me feel better to be *doing* something.

Later that evening, Paula sat drowsily in front of the gently flickering fire. It had been good therapy to keep busy. After she had eaten and bathed, she made the fire and sat in front of it reading for a while. Later, she put some music on the stereo—the Haydn cello concerto—and switched off the lamp.

She was curled up comfortably now on the long couch, gazing at the flames, her eyes half-closed.

She emptied her mind and allowed the music to fill it, responding, as always, to the beautiful sounds that transported her into another world, a world of the spirit where every problem seemed petty and unimportant.

So rapt was she in this private world that she didn't hear Matthew's key in the lock or hear him enter the apartment until some sixth sense told her she was not alone. She opened her eyes and slowly turned her head.

At first, she wasn't sure who it was standing there in the shadows of the darkened room, and her heart gave a great leap of fear. She sat bolt upright, her hand at her throat, her green eyes staring, until he took a step forward and she recognised him in the light of the fire.

'Matthew,' she said with a sigh of relief. 'You startled me. I thought you were out of town.'

He didn't speak. He only stood there staring down at her, his expression unreadable, his face haggard and drawn. Then she remembered what day it was and gave him a closer look. Was he drunk? She wished now she had left when the impulse hit her earlier.

Then he came towards her and sat down on the couch beside her. Her expression was grave.

'I'm very glad to see you, Paula,' he said, his deep voice perfectly steady. 'Have you come to stay?'

He obviously was quite sober. Her spirits soared. 'If you still want me to,' she replied, staring directly into the grey eyes.

'Yes,' he said firmly. 'I want you to. Very much. You know that.' Then he closed his eyes and leaned his head back. 'God, I'm tired,' he said wearily. 'I've been in meetings since early this morning and only just got away.' He opened his eyes then and grinned crookedly. 'I'm also grimy and hungry. Not a great reception for your homecoming, I'm afraid. You've taken me quite by surprise. I'm sorry, Paula. Maybe we can celebrate tomorrow night.'

She watched him as he spoke, her eyes drinking in the dark hair, the broad forehead, the strong straight nose, the firm chin, but most of all the liquid silvery eyes, alight now with genuine pleasure. Great waves of love broke over her. This is where I belong, she thought fiercely. He needs me, and I need him. She put a hand out and laid it on his arm.

'Don't worry about me,' she said softly. 'I'm fine. Why don't you go and clean up and I'll fix you something to eat.' She stood up, tying the blue robe more firmly. 'There isn't much. You'll have to make do with an omelette.'

He loosened his tie and unbuttoned the top button of his shirt, then stretched widely. She stared down at him, mesmerised by the way the strong chest muscles strained against the white shirt, and longed to throw herself into his arms.

He glanced up at her, smiling broadly now. 'That sounds great.'

He stood up and leaned down impulsively to brush her forehead lightly with his lips. When he drew back, their eyes met briefly. He looked away. 'You're a good wife, Mrs Stratton.' His tone was casual, joking. 'I won't be long,' he added as he walked away from her towards his bedroom. 'Give me half an hour.'

As she worked in the kitchen fixing his supper, Paula hummed happily to herself. He seems glad to see me, she thought, as she sliced the ham and beat the eggs. And if the haggard look on his face when she first saw him had been for Beth, it was the sight of *her*, Paula, that had taken it off.

In a little over half an hour she had a tray ready for him and carried it into the living room. He was already there, and she saw him now bent over the fire, stoking it. She watched while he put on another log, then crouched there gazing into the flames, the firelight flickering over his tanned strong features. He had dressed after his shower in a pair of black trousers and a soft grey flannel shirt, open at the neck, the cuffs turned up.

Her throat tightened at the sight of him, and her mouth felt suddenly dry. She loved him so much. If only he could love her, too.

'Here's your supper,' she said in a falsely bright tone as she advanced into the room.

He turned to look at her, the grey eyes following her every movement as she set the tray down on the coffee table in front of the fire. He rose slowly to his feet and came to her side.

'Sit down with me, Paula,' he said. 'Stay with me.'

'Yes, of course.'

While he ate, they chatted about his work, her holiday commission, and what they had both been doing in the past seven weeks. He seemed very hungry and finished every bite of the meal she had prepared for him.

When he had finished she poured coffee for them both. He took his cup and leaned back with a deep sigh of contentment.

'That was wonderful, Paula. I've missed your cooking. Almost as much as I've missed you.'

He was gazing at her now, gravely, holding her eyes in his. A sudden tension had sprung up in the

air between them, and Paula's skin prickled
uneasily. She was uncomfortably aware that all she
had on was the thin blue robe, and she resisted the
impulse to tighten the belt again. She sensed
instinctively that he still desired her, and knew
from her own quickening pulse that if he made one
move towards her, she would be lost.

She thought again of today's date and its
meaning to Matthew. She couldn't allow herself to
be a surrogate for Beth. She could do without
love, she thought, but before she could respond to
Matthew again, she must know that his desire was
for her, and not for a ghost. She made up her
mind, then, set her cup carefully down on the tray
and turned to him.

'You seem to have got through the day much
better this year than last,' she said in a light, brittle
voice.

He frowned. 'I don't understand what you
mean,' he replied with a puzzled look. 'What's so
special about today?' He stared blankly at her.

'It's November the twentieth. Remember? Has it
got any better?'

Then the light suddenly dawned in the grey eyes
as he took in the significance of the date, and the
meaning of her questions. For one split second,
pain flickered in the silvery depths. He shook his
head, set his own cup down, and turned to her.

'I'd forgotten,' he said in a tone of amazed
disbelief. 'It had slipped my mind entirely until
you mentioned it.' Paula held her breath, hardly
daring to hope. He smiled. 'I've been so frantic
about losing you,' he went on, 'scheming how to
get you back, how to keep you, that there's been
no room for anything else.'

'I see,' Paula said in a small voice. 'Well, I'm

back. To stay.' She looked down at her hands, twisting the ties of her robe in her lap and chose her words carefully. 'I want you to know, Matthew, that I understand how you feel. I know you'll always love Beth, that she comes first.' She gave him a direct look. 'You didn't have to put her picture away to spare my feelings.'

He was staring hard at her, his eyes wide, a look of sheer disbelief on his face. 'God, is that what you think?' he breathed. 'I put that picture away weeks ago, right after you left. When I thought I'd lost you for good, I wanted to replace it with one of you, but I couldn't find one. Then I decided to go to Margaret's party after all, to corner you, and *make* you come back, even if I had to carry you off over my shoulder.'

Paula's heart gave a great leap. Was he telling her the truth? Finally, barely able to control the tremor in her voice, she asked simply, 'Why didn't you?'

He gave her a grim look. 'When I walked in and saw you there with Wyatt, laughing, having such a good time, looking so beautiful, I suddenly realised that I had nothing to offer you. All I ever did was make you unhappy. I despised myself for forcing myself on you, half-raping you that last night, for God's sake.'

'I asked for that, Matthew,' she said firmly. 'Besides, I had agreed to have a child.'

He made an abrupt gesture with his hand. 'I know, I know, but I also knew all along it was Richard you loved, and I shouldn't even have made such a request in the first place.'

'Richard!' she exclaimed. 'I don't love Richard.' She reached out a hand and touched his arm. 'Oh, I'll always love him, in a way,' she went on earnestly, 'but Richard is dead. He belongs to the past. You're my husband, now.'

He stared at her, unbelievingly, for a long time. 'Then why did you leave me?' he ground out at last.

She drew her hand away and dropped her eyes to her lap again. 'I couldn't bear it,' she choked out, 'sleeping with you, responding to you, then waking up in the morning and finding you gone.' She looked at him. 'I thought you were using me, to make a baby, as a substitute for the woman you really loved.'

He was shaking his head from side to side. 'I can't believe this,' he said slowly. 'How could two intelligent people operate at such cross-purposes for so long? I left you those times because I wanted to spare you waking up the next morning and seeing I wasn't Richard.'

He leaned slightly towards her then and gave her one long agonised look. He reached out tentatively and with his long, sensitive fingers, lightly touched her hair, her cheek, her lips. She gazed into his eyes, trembling, burning with love and desire. Then, in a swift, sure movement, he gathered her up in his arms, pulling her to him, his face against hers, his mouth at her ear.

'Oh, darling,' he groaned. 'What a fool I've been! I never dreamed I was hurting you. I loved you so much I wanted to save you pain, and all I did was cause it.' He clutched her as if he would never let her go.

She drew her head back and looked up at him. 'You loved me?' she asked breathlessly.

He nodded grimly. 'Almost from the first.' His hands cupped her face. 'You were so different from the others, so remote, so cool, so obviously not interested in me or any other man. And different from Beth, too. I admit she was in my blood for a long time, more a habit, a self-indulgence than anything else.' He smiled. 'And protection, too, from matchmaking matrons.'

'Like Margaret?' she murmured, recalling how her sister had tried so blatantly to throw them together.

'Like Margaret,' he agreed. 'But as soon as I realised that you were really serious about not wanting an emotional involvement, I let down my guard, and from then on all I could think of was getting you on any terms.'

She put a hand up and ran it down the flat plane of his cheek. He had shaved, she could feel, and the skin was warm and smooth to her touch. 'But you were so cold all the time, so remote,' she said, puzzled. 'How was I to know how you felt?'

'I didn't want you to know,' he replied firmly. 'I was afraid if you knew how badly I had fallen for you, I'd frighten you off.'

'Matthew,' she accused, 'do you mean to tell me that your original proposition to join forces and the whole idea of a "platonic" marriage of convenience were all a lie?' Then she gasped as another idea occurred to her. 'And the sudden desire for a child?'

He gave her a wry smile. 'Not entirely. I really did want a child, but I wanted you more.' His arms tightened around her. 'You must understand, darling, that a man in love has no conscience.'

Paula struggled within herself for a moment between indignation and amusement. To deceive her like that! This man was too clever for his own good. He would bear watching in the future. That cool exterior hid a very complex and devious mind. Then she felt his hand moving slowly on her back, his mouth nuzzling softly along her neck, and an irresistible warmth began to spread through her again.

'Forgive me, darling?' he murmured now next to her mouth.

Their eyes met. 'I love you, Matthew,' she whispered. 'There's nothing to forgive.'

With a groan, his mouth hardened on hers, drawing in her lips, then forcing them open, gently, coaxingly. Her arms went around his neck and she lifted herself towards him, aching to feel his hard muscular body next to hers.

She ran her hands up into his dark thick hair, her fingers raking through the crisp strands, every nerve in her body flaming, now, responding to him joyously.

His hands were on her shoulders now, and he tore his mouth away from hers, pushing her away from him slightly so that she was looking up into his eyes, hooded and gleaming with desire. Slowly, his gaze never faltering, his hands slipped down her body, lingering over her straining breasts, bare underneath the thin material of her robe, and then down to fumble with the ties at her waist.

'I want to see you, Paula,' he rasped thickly.

She drew in her breath sharply and nodded, giving him tacit permission to do whatever he wanted with her. She sat motionless, scarcely able to breathe, as he untied the robe, then reached up to slip it off her shoulders and down her arms until it fell loosely around her waist.

Her skin burned under his hungry gaze, and she lifted her chin slightly to mask the sudden shyness. His hands reached out to cover her breasts, the strong tapering fingers moulding the soft fullness.

She moaned deep in her throat as his thumbs began circling around and around the taut nipples, her momentary embarrassment gone in the sheer pleasure of his warm touch.

Then, almost in a frenzy, she began to unbutton his shirt, until his chest was bare. Moving the folds of material aside, she leaned down to touch the warm bare skin of his chest with her lips. She could feel the sudden rapid beating of his heart and the strong muscles quiver under her mouth as it moved over his body.

He stood up, then, bringing her with him. The robe fell to her feet and she stood before him in the dim light of the slowly dying fire. Shrugging quickly out of his shirt, he gathered her to him, crushing her breasts against his strong bare chest.

'Let's go to bed, darling,' he murmured at her ear.

The fire was barely flickering by now, and they made their way in almost total darkness down the hall to her bedroom. Matthew guided her from behind, pressed closely up against her, his arms firmly around her waist.

When they reached the side of the bed, one hand come up to move lightly, tantalisingly over her breasts, and the other slid downward over her stomach, her hips, her thighs. By the light of the pale full moon shining dimly in through the sheer curtains at the bedroom window, she could see his hands travelling over her body, heightening the pleasure of his touch to an almost frightening intensity.

Moaning deep in her throat, she leaned back against him in a mindless ecstasy, giving herself up completely to the exploring fingers and the shafts of sheer sensuous pleasure coursing through her.

Slowly, he turned her around to face him, and his arms enfolded her closely, gently, protectively, for several long moments. Then he looked down into her eyes.

'I love you, Paula,' he said. 'I want you more than I've ever wanted anything in my life. I was dead inside, and you've brought me back to life.'

'I love you, too, Matthew,' she breathed. 'So much more than I ever dreamed possible.'

She hesitated for a second, then, daringly, her fingers began to fumble at the buckle of his belt. His hands dropped loosely to his sides, and he stood motionless, looking down at her as she tugged at the black trousers, pulling them down over his lean hips and long legs.

When he stepped out of the trousers, she ran her hands back up slowly along the muscled legs, covered with coarse hair, over the flat hard stomach, until, once again, her arms twined around his neck and she arched her body up closely to his, joyously aware of his hard aching need of her.

With a groan, his arms came around her, his lips claimed hers once again, his tongue thrusting, probing the soft interior of her mouth, and they sank slowly on to the bed.

When they came together at last, this time Paula could give herself to him totally, meeting his pulsing need with wild abandon, secure now in the knowledge that he loved her completely.

Paula awoke the next morning to the pale November sunshine spilling into the bedroom through the thin curtains at the window.

She stretched luxuriously, still half-asleep, sated with pleasurable content. As she moved, she felt a heaviness on her body, and suddenly became aware of an arm thrown across her, a large hand clasping her possessively around the waist.

Memory came flooding back, and with a little smile, she glanced down at the dark head of her sleeping husband burrowed in her neck, his long body curled against her. She could feel his even breath on her skin, the steady heartbeat under her arm.

Carefully, so as not to disturb him and shatter the precious moment, she reached over and gently smoothed the dark hair, tousled over his forehead now in sleep. He stirred slightly, and the hand on her waist tightened as he shifted closer to her, his mouth nuzzling the hollow of her neck under her jaw.

Then he opened his eyes, blinked, and looked up at her, smiling. 'Good morning, darling,' he said in a low voice. He raised himself up on one elbow and bent down to kiss her lightly on the mouth.

The hand began moving now, travelling over her breast. She reached out and held it firmly in place.

'Before you get too engrossed in *that*,' she said firmly, 'I have a question to ask you.'

His mouth was at her breast now. 'Ask away,' he murmured against it.

'How would you like to be a father?' she asked quickly. His mouth was creating a disturbance in her bloodstream, and soon it would be too late for discussion.

'Mmm,' he said. 'Any time you like.'

Now his tongue was making circles on her other breast, and she knew she was almost lost. She put her arms around his broad, strong back and held him tightly.

'How about roughly seven months from now?' she said with a sigh of contentment.

His mouth stilled for a moment, then abruptly the dark head came up. He stared down at her.

'What did you say?'

'Ah,' she said with a smile. 'That got your attention, didn't it?'

'Do you mean it?' She nodded gravely.

He gathered her into his arms and held her close, and as she nestled contentedly against him, her heart almost bursting with love and joy, she thought about the habit of loving, as necessary to her existence as breathing, and turned her head to welcome her husband's kiss.

ANNE MATHER

Anne Mather, one of Harlequin's leading romance authors, has published more than 100 million copies worldwide, including **Wild Concerto**, a *New York Times* best-seller.

Catherine Loring was an innocent in a South American country beset by civil war. Doctor Armand Alvares was arrogant yet compassionate. They could not ignore the flame of love igniting within them…whatever the cost.

HIDDEN IN THE FLAME

❧Harlequin❧

Tender, captivating stories
that sweep to faraway
places and delight with the
magic of love.

Exciting romance novels
for the woman of today—a
rare blend of passion and
dramatic realism.

Sensual and romantic
stories about choices,
dilemmas, resolutions, and
above all, the fulfillment
of love.

GEN-A-2

Harlequin
is romance...

INDULGE IN THE PLEASURE OF SUPERB ROMANCE READING BY CHOOSING THE MOST POPULAR LOVE STORIES IN THE WORLD

Longer, more absorbing love stories for the connoisseur of romantic fiction.

Contemporary romances— uniquely North American in flavor and appeal.

An innovative series blending contemporary romance with fast-paced adventure.

and you can never have too much romance.